P9-DBP-348

BLAIRSVILLE SENIOR HIGH SCHOOL
BLAIRSVILLE, PENNA.

Burning Secrets

manuscript 2/11 *No*

BURNING SECRETS

■

G. N. HELD

AVALON BOOKS
THOMAS BOUREGY AND COMPANY, INC.
401 LAFAYETTE STREET
NEW YORK, NEW YORK 10003

©Copyright 1991 by G. N. Held
Library of Congress Catalog Card Number: 91-92093
ISBN 0-8034-8881-5
All rights reserved.
All the characters in this book are fictitious,
and any resemblance to actual persons,
living or dead, is purely coincidental.

PRINTED IN THE UNITED STATES OF AMERICA
ON ACID-FREE PAPER
BY HADDON CRAFTSMEN, SCRANTON, PENNSYLVANIA

This book is lovingly dedicated to my family and friends, both those with me now and those deeply missed. Though I provided the words, you provided the soul.

Chapter One

It wasn't the flames or the heat or even the helplessness of the situation that scared her. It was the *sound* of the fire that did it, the hissing and crackling as it devoured everything in its way. A sound like that meant that soon she would be either very dead or very lucky. Third-generation police officer Sarah Phillips prayed she would be the latter.

"Where are you?" she called above the noise as she made her way up the apartment-building stairs. No answer. The smoke was starting to filter up, and she knew there was precious little time to find the missing children.

"Where are you?" she called again, her flashlight shining eerily through the corridor. Quickly she found the apartment they were last seen in and tried the door. It was locked. She used the key the superintendent had given her, but the door swung in

1

only a few inches, stopped by a strong chain. Looking into the apartment, she could see two small boys huddled together.

"I'm a police officer—take off the chain!" she yelled, but they didn't move. Knowing further coaxing would be both time-consuming and pointless, she threw her body against the door. It didn't open.

Gathering her strength, Sarah kicked against the solid wood. The chain gave, but so did her leg. She tumbled into the room, pain racing through her.

Don't think about it, she told herself, and got up slowly. The fearful look on the boys' faces and the growing sound of the fire kept her from succumbing to the agony playing at the edge of her mind.

She took a step forward, but her ankle wouldn't support her. She noticed a baseball bat in the corner, and motioned for the older boy to bring it over. She found she could walk if she used it as a cane.

"Let's go." Sarah moved toward the door, but only the older child followed. The other stood and cried.

"What are your names?" she asked the older boy.

"I'm Jim and he's Robert," he said. "He's scared."

Who isn't? Sarah thought, and bent down to face the sobbing child. "Robert, everything's going to be fine," she said as soothingly as she could. "Your mommy is waiting outside, and I'm going to take you to her. You'd like that, wouldn't you?''

Robert nodded and Sarah smiled, listening all the while for the sounds of the fire engines she feared would not come. She had been the first to arrive at the burning semiabandoned building. Upon hearing of the missing children, she had raced into the flames, not wanting to waste precious minutes waiting for the fire department to arrive. It all seemed like ages ago.

"Good boy, Robert," she continued. "Now give me your hand and we'll show everyone how brave you are."

Slowly the boy reached forward and Sarah pulled him into an embrace. Unfortunately, Robert wouldn't let go and there was no time to pry him loose. Sarah stood up, holding the child with one arm and leaning on the bat with the other. It was uncomfortable, but workable.

"Follow me," she commanded Jim and went back into the hallway, which was now completely filled with smoke. Both boys started coughing, and she ripped her handkerchief in half. She gave a piece to each child, telling him to hold it over his mouth and nose.

The trio made their way to the staircase, only to find that the fire had spread. They weren't able to go down, and Sarah knew that if the firemen hadn't gotten to them by now, they never would in time to save them. They were on their own, with only one way to go—up.

Sarah and the children climbed up the two remaining flights of stairs to the door leading to the roof. Once there, she made a horrible discovery: The door was bolted shut.

Sarah put Robert down and, shifting all her weight to her good leg, swung the bat at the bolt. It was a home-run swing, but futile. Another frustrated swing brought the same result.

"I know another way!" Jim yelled. He led her to a nearby utility room and pointed to a small grate. "We can get out through there!"

Sarah looked at the grate and knew she'd never fit through. The boys would make it, though, and, at the moment, that was all that mattered. She punched out the grate with the bat. Cold night air, along with the sound of a helicopter, swept in. She looked up to see the welcome sight of a police rescue squad hovering overhead. She shone her light in an SOS pattern and was relieved to see a ladder fall from the helicopter.

"When you get up there, go to the ladder and they'll tell you what to do," Sarah said to the boys. "I have to go back and try to shoot the bolt off, so stay away from the door, understand?"

Both boys nodded and she helped them escape

through the hole. After they had disappeared, Sarah went back to the roof door. It was almost impossible to see and extremely difficult to breathe. From below, the sounds of the building falling apart could be heard over the fire's crackling. Sarah inspected the bolt and fired her gun at the stress point. All six shots were perfect, but the bolt still held. Quickly, she reloaded and tried again. This time the bolt flew apart and the door swung outward.

With the door open, the smoke rushed out, carrying Sarah with it. She fell down hard on the rooftop, the pain roaring back into her. The sight of the swaying helicopter ladder just a few yards distant gave her the strength to throw off the pain once more. She limped toward it and was no fewer than two feet away when the roof below her gave out and her bad leg crashed through. She screamed in agony, then in horror, as she saw the helicopter begin to pull away and heard the ominous sound of the flames coming closer and closer . . . .

Sarah sat bolt upright, her body covered with sweat, and groaned as she looked at her clock: eight P.M. She had stayed awake the entire night and most of the morning, in order to get accustomed to the hours her new job called for. But all her planning was for nothing, as the fire dream made what little sleep she had managed to get seem like none.

She went to the bathroom and hopped into the shower, hoping to cleanse away the dirt she felt in body and mind. She stayed there until the hot water ran out, but it didn't help. Shutting her eyes tight, she went through the exercise the doctors had taught her.

"Think it out. Think it out," she repeated, and continued in her mind with the reality that was the rest of the dream.

Back on the roof, Sarah had managed to free her leg and crawl to the building's edge. She saw that the fire department had set up a net far below. She said a prayer and was about to jump when the helicopter, which had been forced to change position because of a shift in the wind, returned. She grabbed on to its ladder and was pulled to safety moments before the entire structure collapsed.

The weeks that followed brought honors and headlines, and then medical tests and, ultimately, a discharge from the job she loved so much. "Can't fight crime if you can't run," they said and, though she hated to admit it, she knew they were right. If only she hadn't gone into . . . . No!

Sarah shook out of it and found she was staring at her reflection in the mirror. Her short auburn hair was flat against her head, her brown eyes were bloodshot, and her strong features were puffy from lack of sleep. Even her lithe, athletic body seemed all wrong.

You look like I feel, she said to herself, groaning.

Usually, playing out the apartment-building fire made her feel better, but it didn't work now. Tonight was her first night as evening security chief at New Idea Labs in the suburbs of New Jersey.

Sarah looked at herself again in the mirror. More than a year of intensive physical and mental therapy had been necessary to help her heal. She wasn't about to give up now.

Chapter Two

Sarah parked her car near the front entrance of New Idea Labs, took a deep breath of the hot summer night air, and walked across the neatly manicured grounds. As she got closer, the main doors opened and a big, uniformed man walked out.

"Hi, I'm Sarah Phillips," she said and extended her hand. "I'm the new—"

"Bill Morton," the man interrupted her gruffly. He shook her hand, then pointed over her shoulder. "You can't park there. Those spots are reserved for laboratory personnel."

She turned to look at her car, one of only a half dozen or so in the huge lot.

"All right," she said, not wanting any trouble, especially on her first day. "Where should I park?"

"Security parks over in the far lot." He indicated an area off in the distance. "My space is number sixty-two, but you can't have it until I'm officially retired. Up until then, I suppose, you can park in the handicapped spot.''

"No, I can't," Sarah said firmly. "I'm not handicapped."

"Your license plate says otherwise." His eyes took her in. "And so did the police department, from what I heard. That's nothing to be ashamed about— I heard you did a real brave thing. You should be proud of yourself."

Sarah didn't know how to handle this man. One second he was cross with her, the next he was all praise.

"I did what had to be done," she said. "Now, Mr. Morton, if you'll please tell me where I can park, I'll move my car and we can get to work."

"Suit yourself." He shrugged. "Space ninety-four is unassigned. You can use that until I train you and retire. And call me Morty." He turned and went back inside the main facility.

Sarah returned to her car, drove to the other lot, and parked. It was a long way back and the pain in her leg started to flare, but she walked quickly, determined that no one would question her ability to do this job. Morty buzzed her in through the smoked-glass front doors and was waiting behind a huge oval command center just inside.

"This is where it all happens," he said as she

came around to see the interior, which was filled with television monitors, recording machines, and indicators of all types. None of this was visible from the other side.

"Wow," Sarah whispered.

"That was my first reaction too, and there was a whole lot less when I first started," Morty said. "Don't worry, though, you'll figure out what everything means once you're here for a while."

"I hope so." Sarah couldn't believe the security they had. She knew New Idea had important government and industrial projects going on, but she hadn't thought it would be this well protected.

"What you have to remember is that New Idea attracts scientists and projects not only because of its equipment but also because of its reputation for safety, security, and privacy." Morty seemed to anticipate her questions. "Recently it was decided that, to further enhance our image, we would keep the facility open twenty-four hours a day, seven days a week, three hundred sixty-five days a year. Scientists need to have access to their work around the clock, and we have to accommodate them."

"Good idea," Sarah said, feeling the need to say something.

"We'll see." Morty shrugged noncommittally. "Anyway, it increased our need for security personnel. That's another reason why you're here." He got up and put the alarm systems on automatic. "It's too soon to go over particulars, so let's get a cup of coffee. After that, we'll walk around and you can start to familiarize yourself with the surroundings."

"Sounds good," she said.

After a cup of coffee, they began to tour the facilities. New Idea Labs was filled with quiet wonders. From the dark, yet warm, decor of the corridors, to the comfortable-looking recliners in the lounge, the place gave off a homey feeling rather than the stark, sterile atmosphere she had expected. Even Morty seemed nicer than he had been outside. For the first time since her accident, Sarah felt as if she were in a place where she belonged. It was a very good feeling.

They stopped in front of a locked lab with a harsh-looking, starkly lettered sign pasted across it that read, AUTHORIZED PERSONNEL ONLY. It was very out of place in the otherwise cozy atmosphere. Sarah turned to Morty for an explanation.

"This is Dr. Pornaygun's lab," he said, his demeanor serious. "Under no circumstance is anyone but the doctor and his two assistants allowed to enter it."

"What's in there?" Sarah ventured tentatively.

"The rumor is they're working on an alternative energy source, but that's not our concern. It doesn't matter what it is: As long as it's here, our job is to keep it safe.''

''I see.''

Morty shook his head. ''No, you don't, but over time, you will. Right now, just remember what I said about who's allowed in there. Even if there's a fire, you call one of the three scientists before you do anything else. If they aren't available, I have a special number for you to call.'' Morty stopped talking as he saw a vacant look creep into Sarah's eyes. ''Sarah? Are you listening to me?''

''Yes, yes,'' she said quickly. When he had mentioned fire, her mind had filled with memories of the apartment building. With an effort, she returned her thoughts to the present. ''No one goes in there for any reason, except the doctor and his assistants,'' she repeated.

Satisfied that she was paying attention, Morty nodded, and then they moved on.

The rest of the tour was uneventful, and Sarah was back to normal long before they returned to the command center. A man about Sarah's age was waiting for them as they arrived. He seemed to be very happy.

''Morty, I bet if the board knew how pretty your replacement would be, they would have retired you years ago.'' The man smiled at Sarah as he spoke. ''Hi, I'm Ron Dancer. You must be Sarah Phillips.''

"Yes, I am." She extended her hand, which Ron shook in both of his.

"Ron is one of Dr. Pornaygun's assistants," Morty said, not looking very happy.

"Nice to meet you, Ron."

Ron gave her a mock bow. "The pleasure is all mine." Despite Morty's obvious dislike for him, Sarah couldn't help but be charmed by Ron's good looks and comfortable banter. He looked like the boy next door, all grown up.

"Don't you have somewhere to go?" Morty asked Ron. "I think I hear Pornaygun calling you."

Ron continued smiling as he looked at the soon-to-retire night security chief. "It's the wonderful moments like this that I'm going to miss when you're gone," he said, and Sarah had to stifle a giggle. Ron took her hand again. "Good luck, Sarah, and if there's anything I can ever do for you, please don't hesitate to call." He winked at her, saluted Morty, and sauntered away down the corridor.

"Stay away from that one," Morty grumbled after Ron had left.

"He doesn't seem that bad," Sarah said, half to herself.

"He is, and the other one's even worse!"

Did Sarah detect something in his voice? "In what way?" she asked, wanting to know what was going on.

"In every way," Morty snarled. Then his tone and attitude lightened. "All right, it's only a feeling on my part, but my advice to you is to give them both a wide berth."

"Okay," she said, not wanting to pursue the situation any further, but making a mental note of the conversation. Morty dropped the subject as well.

The next few hours were spent looking over the various features of the command center. There was a lot to learn, but Sarah saw that everything followed logical steps that she was sure she could master. After a while, Morty took her to the lounge to see a company video. He turned off the lights, and put them on a timer to coincide with the tape's running time.

The surprisingly entertaining video showed the history of New Idea Labs. The lab, in its original location, had been formed almost twenty years ago by a consortium of scientists looking for a home for their advanced experiments. They came up with a number of profitable ideas that enabled them to build this facility. Here, they could provide state-of-the-art labs and equipment to even more scientists, in return for a percentage of any profits. It was a partnership that worked well for all concerned.

As the tape ended and the lights turned on automatically, Sarah heard a noise in the lounge behind her. She whirled around to see someone trying to sneak out.

"Hold it right there!" she ordered, and the figure, already half out of the lounge, stopped. "Now back into the room with your hands where I can see them."

The man put up his hands and did as ordered. "I can explain—" he began.

"Quiet!" Sarah interrupted, and sized him up. He was roughly Ron's height, a few inches taller than she, but where the other man was of average size, this one was heavily muscled. She made him stay facing away from her so he couldn't tell she was unarmed. "Who are you, and what are you doing here?"

"I just came in for a cup of coffee. You can see it on the counter," he said.

"If you came in for it, then why were you sneaking off without it?" she asked, not satisfied with his answer.

"I didn't want to disturb you, so I decided to leave when the lights came on. I'm sorry if I scared you."

"You didn't scare me," she said firmly, "and you still haven't told me who you are."

"I'm Sinclair Edwards. I work here at New Idea with Dr. Pornaygun. If you'll let me, I'll show you my identification. It's in my pocket."

"All right," Sarah said. "But do it slowly."

"Of course." He did as she said, his identification proving his claim.

Sarah groaned softly and handed back his badge.

"Everything seems to be in order," she said, embarrassed over the situation her police instincts had placed her in.

"Can I put my hands down?" he asked in a somewhat amused tone.

"Yes. I'm sorry about this. You see, this is my first day. . . . " He turned around and, even though she had glanced briefly at his picture on the badge, it didn't prepare her for seeing him in reality. His features were dark and strong, but it was his eyes that made him stand out. They were the eyes of a poet or a dreamer and radiated a life of their own. After a moment, she realized that not only was she staring at him but he was staring back at her too. A feeling passed through her, the strangest one she had ever experienced.

"Who are you?" he asked in a soft half whisper. His eyes twinkled like small stars. Before she could find the words to answer, Morty entered and scowled at both of them.

"What's going on here?" he asked Sarah. "He giving you any trouble?"

Sarah managed to break away from the man's gaze and compose herself. "No. No trouble at all. Just an unfortunate case of mistaken identity."

Morty looked at Sinclair Edwards. "Is that right?"

"Yes," he answered, still looking at Sarah. "If

you'll excuse me, I have to get back to work.'' He vanished with a grace that belied his size.

"Seems like I got here in the nick of time," Morty said, seeing the expression on Sarah's face as she watched him go. "Don't let Sin Edwards fool you, Sarah. He's no good. Him and that smart-mouth Ron—they're trouble through and through!'' Sarah said nothing and Morty sighed. "I suppose you'll have to find out the hard way, then.''

She shrugged and they returned to the command center, where her lessons on the various systems continued. Soon it was morning and her first day was over. She said good-bye to Morty and went out to her car. Up ahead, at the start of the parking lot, she spotted Sin.

"Sin!'' she called out impulsively, and walked as quickly as she could to meet him. He turned to stare at her, and she groped for what to say. "I . . . I want to apologize for before.''

His gaze left her with that strange feeling again. "Apology accepted,'' he said. "You're the new night security chief, aren't you?''

"Yes, I'm Sarah Phillips.'' They shook hands and, as his hand engulfed hers, Sarah felt the power yet gentleness of his touch. The handshake lasted a few seconds longer than it should have, and they both let go feeling a bit awkward.

"I—I suppose I'd better be going," she said. "It's been a long night."

"The first one is always the hardest." Sin glanced off in the distance.

"Are you waiting for someone?"

"Yes," he said, and Sarah felt disappointed and then surprised at her feelings. She had hardly known the man more than a few hours, nor had she said more than a few dozen words to him, and she was upset that someone was picking him up.

"There's my ride now." Sin pointed to a new model sports car pulling into the lot. It came to a halt in front of them and Ron stuck his head out the window.

"Hi, Sarah." He smiled broadly at her. "How was your first night?"

"Interesting," she managed to say, feeling better that Sin was waiting for Ron.

"Sin and I are going to get some breakfast," Ron said. "Why don't you join us?"

"Well, I don't—"

"I won't take no for an answer." Ron's smile even broadened as he opened the car door for her.

"I don't know if that's such a good idea," Sin said, looking at Ron. "Sarah's tired and we have a lot to discuss about the project."

Ron waved Sin off. "So we don't discuss it for once. It's Sarah's first day and she's been cooped up with Morty all night long. The very least we can do is treat her to the finest breakfast New Jersey has to offer.''

Sin shrugged and got into the backseat, while Sarah got in the front. Ron drove into town, keeping the conversation going with amusing stories about places he'd been and people he'd known. Sin, on the other hand, kept quiet, though his eyes took in everything around him.

"So what about you, Sarah?" Ron asked as they sipped their coffee in a local diner. "How did you wind up at New Idea?"

Sarah didn't really want to talk about it, but felt as though she had to. "There's not much to tell," she began. "I used to be a police officer, but I hurt my leg in an accident and had to retire. Some people on the force recommended me to New Idea Labs, and here I am."

"Are you all right now?" Sin asked, speaking for the first time since they got into the car.

"Yes, I'm fine." She was surprised at how genuinely concerned he was.

"Our sphinxlike friend here has quite a story to tell too." Ron slapped Sin on the back in a good-natured gesture.

Sin looked upset. "Ron, don't—"

"Oh, come on, Sin," Ron said, then leaned across the table. "It was a dark and dreary night and there—"

"Okay, okay—if it has to be told, *I'll* tell it," Sin interrupted the other man's melodramatics. "It was nothing more than being in the wrong place at the right time. Some chemicals caught fire at a lab I was visiting, and I went in and pulled out two people. It was no big deal—it was only a small blaze and the fire department would have rescued them if I hadn't."

"It was still brave of you," Sarah said, and she meant it, even though she didn't feel the same way about her own rescue.

"It really was nothing," Sin insisted.

"Well, it would have been something if *I* had told it!" Ron exclaimed, and they all laughed.

When they left the restaurant they drove back to New Idea to drop Sarah off. By then the parking lots were filled with the day shift workers' cars. As she headed for her own car, Sarah felt good about her first day and the promise the future held. That all changed as she opened her car door and a note fell out. *Stay away from them,* it read, and she knew it came from Morty. She folded it up and put it in her pocket.

Nothing's ever easy, she thought, and headed for home.

Chapter Three

Morty's retirement party was two weeks away, and Sarah was nervous. It wasn't because she felt she couldn't handle the job—even Morty himself was confident she could—it was because she didn't have a date for the affair. She felt foolish worrying about something so juvenile, but she worried nevertheless.

And it wasn't as though she'd never had a date. Before she had joined the force, Sarah had been extremely popular with men. But after she became a policewoman, things had changed.

Being an officer was the culmination of a lifetime's worth of work. Her father and grandfather had been detectives, and that was her ultimate goal. She took every "dirty" assignment there was and worked countless hours of overtime in order to meet her goal. It was not exactly a situation conducive to keeping up a sustained romance, so she had put that part of her life on hold. Now that her police career was over, she wanted her life to return to normal.

She was apprehensive about something else too: Sin Edwards. In the weeks she had been working at New Idea, Sarah had come to respect the handsome scientist more and more. No, respect wasn't the right word—she was infatuated with him. Although their conversations lasted only a few minutes each, she felt very much attracted to him.

At first, she felt her attitude was very shallow. How could she possibly feel this way about someone she had barely spoken to? After some introspection, she came up with the answer. Even though she had not actually talked with Sin all that much, she still knew what he was like. Because of her duties at the command center, she had observed all his conversations with the people who worked nights. She learned he was a kind and understanding man, although soft-spoken and somewhat shy.

Sarah knew Morty was aware of her infatuation, but after that first day he never had brought up the subject again. She was both thankful and regretful for that; thankful that she didn't have to defend herself and her thoughts, but regretful because Morty had become a true friend and she would have liked to talk with him about her situation.

To complicate matters further, there was Ron Dancer. Right from the start, he had gone out of his way to be friendly. Initially, Sarah was happy for the attention, but after a while, she tried to avoid him. It wasn't that she disliked Ron, she just didn't think of him in the same way she thought of Sin. She also wanted to leave the way open for Sin, in case he wanted to ask her to the retirement party. It was, however, getting closer to the event, and it didn't look like the situation was going to change.

On the monitors, Sarah traced Ron's progress as he came out of his lab, and she realized he was headed for her. It was Morty's break and she groaned, knowing she was stuck here since the command center had to be staffed at all times. She was sure Ron was going to ask her to the party. She was wrong.

"Have you seen Sin tonight?" he asked, smiling a little less than usual.

She shook her head, and for a fleeting moment, Ron actually seemed to frown.

"There's nothing wrong, is there?" she asked, puzzled.

Ron shrugged. "I don't think so—at least, I hope not. Sin told me he'd be a little late tonight, but it's been three hours already. He's never been this late." Ron's serious mood turned upbeat abruptly. "Oh, well, I'm sure he'll be here soon. If not, I'll call him at home later."

Sarah had her own thoughts on the matter.

"Maybe I should call him now." She was both worried that something might have happened to Sin, and happy for the opportunity to speak with him.

"That might not be a bad idea," Ron agreed. "Although he'll probably pull up here any minute."

Sarah didn't want to look too eager. "You're probably right, but it won't hurt to give him a ring." She punched up the file of employee telephone numbers and scanned it until she got to *Edwards, Sinclair*.

"You're a true credit to the security profession in particular, and humanity in general." Ron gave her a thumbs up as he walked away. "Call me if you find out anything."

Sarah dialed Sin's home. All she got was an answering machine.

"Sin, this is Sarah Phillips at New Idea," she said after the tone. "It's one A.M. and we wanted to make sure—" Suddenly the phone, lights, and all the electrical equipment went dead, followed almost instantaneously by a distant yet loud explosion outside the lab. Moments after, the emergency generator sprang to life and some of the lights came back on. The phone remained out. Sarah quickly shut off all nonessential equipment.

"Take a physical check of the west wing!" Morty yelled, running back from the lounge. "I'll take the east. I'll meet you back here in five minutes."

Sarah jumped up and ran down the corridor as fast

as she could. Her leg started to tingle a bit, but held up under the strain. Though her heart raced, she felt confident she could handle this emergency.

There were seven labs on the west wing. She inspected the first six and found them empty for the night and showing no signs of trouble. The seventh lab was Pornaygun's, and Sarah knocked on the closed door until Ron came out. He was wearing a pair of goggles around his neck and didn't seem to be particularly alarmed at what was happening.

"What can I do for you?" he asked.

"Ron, don't you know what's going on? The lights and power have all gone out—we're on emergency systems!" She pointed down the corridor, where only a few scattered lights were on. Ron looked at them, then back at her.

"I didn't know," he said. "I was welding, and that doesn't work off the electrical system. What can I do to help?"

"Turn off everything that's not essential and meet me at the command center," Sarah ordered, then headed back to the rendezvous point. Morty was just arriving, looking grimmer than usual.

"Everything's all right in the east," he reported.

"From the west also. Any idea what that explosion was?" she asked.

"No, and our phone systems are still down. Maybe now the board will take my cellular-phone suggestion seriously. We're so isolated out here, the authorities might not even be aware that anything's wrong.''

''Then I'll have to go and alert them,'' Sarah said firmly. ''You stay here and make sure everything stays status quo.''

''It might be dangerous out there,'' Morty warned. ''I'll go.''

''It might be dangerous here,'' Sarah countered. ''Besides, you know this place inside out. It makes sense for me to go.''

Morty frowned. ''Sarah, it's raining outside, and with you not knowing the roads . . . .''

''I know the roads,'' a voice said, and they turned to see Ron standing behind them. ''I'll drive.''

''No, this is our responsibility,'' Morty told him.

''That's ridiculous,'' Ron said. ''Besides, what if all this is a plot to break in here? Either way I stand to be in danger, so why not let me do some good?''

Morty thought that over. ''Go ahead,'' he said begrudgingly, ''but be careful. Both of you!''

''Will do,'' Sarah assured him, glad for some action. ''Let's go, Ron!''

As soon as they were outside, it was obvious where the trouble was. The rain and darkness around them were near absolute except for a flickering light off in the distance.

"I'll get my car," Ron said, and disappeared into the blackness.

A few moments later Sarah heard the roar of his car engine, then saw the lights go on like some sleeping giant come to life. The vehicle raced toward her, its headlights illuminating the moisture on the ground and in the air. The car screeched to a halt, and she jumped in.

Ron sped out of the parking lot and down the road toward the light. The highway was winding, dark, and slick, but Ron handled the car well, showing that he had traveled this route many times before.

"I have a feeling it might be the transformer," he said as they got closer to the source.

"Maybe," Sarah agreed. Then a voice in her head called out the word "fire" and she fell into a moody silence.

Soon they arrived at the scene and, though she was relieved to see there was no fire, the situation didn't call for any celebration. A car had crashed into a transmission tower and one of the power cables had broken off. It lay twitching across the top of the tower, giving off a showering cascade of sparks.

Ron stopped the car a safe distance away and grabbed Sarah's arm as she tried to get out.

"Are you crazy?" he yelled at her. "That line could come down at any second!"

She pushed his arm away. "There might be people

in there. If the line comes down and hits that car, they'll be electrocuted!''

Ron grabbed hold of her again, this time tighter than before. "And so will you if you're out there!"

Her eyes pierced his with forceful intensity. "I have to do it."

He still held on. "Down the road there has to be a switch that will cut off all the power. I can—"

"Then go do it." With a circular motion, Sarah pulled free of his grasp. She jumped out of the car and ran toward the other one, keeping her head down to avoid the rain of sparks. She didn't even hear Ron as he zoomed off.

The sparks burned her as she went, but she put the pain aside. She was getting good at doing that. Although it was dark out, the twitching light overhead gave off an eerie glow that let her see into the crashed vehicle. There was no one inside.

"Hello! Hello!" she called into the surrounding area, but there was no response. She turned away and was about to search for the occupants when the cable fell a few more feet. Awkwardly she tried to get out of the way, but she twisted her bad leg. She fell to the ground, the lights she now saw created by pain rather than sparks. Although her brain knew she had to move, her body didn't respond.

We've got you, she heard a voice say, and looked

up to see the boys from the apartment building. They were on fire and grinning down at her.

"No!" she yelled, and started to thrash about.

"Hold still, Sarah!" a voice roared, and the boys' faces melded together and turned into Sin. "I've got you!" Sin picked her up as though she weighed nothing and began to move away from the scene.

What happened next was in slow motion. As Sin carried her, the cable wrenched loose and, like a cracking whip, reared back and came lashing out at them, its tip spitting out electrical death.

Sin was running as fast as he could and was out of range of the cable itself, but an arc of electricity knifed through the air and stabbed him in the back. Sarah was thrown from his grasp and landed a few feet away, out of reach of the snapping current.

Although it lasted only the briefest of seconds, the picture of Sin, his body shaking and outlined by light, would last in her memory forever. Then, as quickly as it began, the electricity turned off and Sin slumped to the ground, seemingly holding out his arms to her. Sarah reached out to him, then the pain overwhelmed her and she blacked out.

With a terrible suddenness, she came back to consciousness and the world around was illuminated. It took a moment, but then she realized that someone was calling her name and the light was coming from the headlights of a car that was pointed at her.

"Sarah! It's me, Ron!" the voice said, and she used it as an anchor to pull herself back to reality. Her leg was throbbing, but the brunt of the pain had subsided. There would be time to worry about herself later. She looked around quickly and saw Sin lying on the ground, just outside the circle of light.

"Forget about me," she said, pointing at Sin. Ron's face grew drawn and white as he scrambled over to his fallen colleague. Sarah crawled over to see Ron holding his friend's head in his lap. Sin was breathing and his eyes were open, but they showed no sign of the intelligence that had so animated them before.

"Say something!" Ron snapped his fingers in Sin's face. He didn't respond and Ron turned to Sarah. "What happened?"

Her words came in gulps, but she managed to get the story out about how Sin had saved her from the falling cable, getting hit in the process.

Ron moaned. "If only I had turned off the electricity sooner!"

"You did the best you could," Sarah consoled him, her heart beating wildly as she looked at Sin's semiconscious form. "He looks like he's in shock, and there's—" She stopped as Sin began to groan and understanding returned to his eyes. He turned his head to focus on her.

"Are you all right?" he asked hoarsely, his first thoughts of her.

A lump caught in her throat. "I'm fine—you saved my life." She crawled closer. "But forget about me. It's you we're concerned about."

"I'm fine," he insisted, though he was obviously still groggy. "I was shocked for a moment, that's all."

In the distance came the sound of sirens. Help was on the way, but it would be another few minutes.

"I'd better make sure they can spot us," Ron said. He got up and moved his car so that the headlights were shining down the road, leaving Sin and Sarah in the dark.

"You saved my life," she repeated, her voice a whisper as she took his hand. "I won't forget that."

"It was nothing." He squeezed her hand, and despite her pain, Sarah couldn't help but feel good. "Someday you can save mine."

"Don't make light of it," she continued. "If you hadn't come along I'd be—"

"Don't even think it," Sin whispered. "We're okay, and that's all that counts. Sarah, I—"

Ron picked that time to return. "They should be here any minute," he interrupted. "I wonder where the driver of that other car went to?"

Sarah's thoughts reluctantly turned back to the

situation at hand. "That's a good question," she said.

Ron turned to Sin and looked at him in what Sarah thought was an odd way. "Sin, how did you know to come up here and find us?" he asked.

"I was in town when I heard the explosion," Sin told him, his voice back to normal. "I could tell it came from up here, and I had a feeling it was at the lab."

"Then the power didn't go off where you were?" Ron asked, and Sarah wondered what he was driving at.

"No. I heard the explosion, dropped everything I was doing, and rushed out here. Luckily, I arrived in time to see that cable coming down toward Sarah. I'm glad I did."

"So am I," Sarah said, and as her eyes met Sin's, she felt something pass between them that sent shivers through her.

"What about the—" Ron was interrupted by the arriving emergency squads. The various firefighters, police, and ambulance personnel swarmed over them, and they had to tell their stories over and over again. There was no sign of the other car's passengers, and a check by the police found that it had been stolen.

The medical team decided to admit Sin to a local hospital for observation, and he was put on a stretcher despite his protests. Sarah had only twisted her leg, but was told to come down to the hospital for X rays after she finished speaking to the police.

"I'll take you," Ron offered, then turned to Sin, who was about to be wheeled away. "Sin, you said you rushed over here when you heard the explosion. Is there somebody waiting for you? Were you on a date?"

Sarah turned to see a red-faced Sin. "No, I was . . . . Yes, I was on a date," he said softly, and Sarah's heart sank. "You don't have to call her, though. I told her not to wait." Then Sin was hustled onto the ambulance and whisked away.

On their way to the hospital, after all the questioning was over, Ron asked Sarah to go to Morty's retirement party with him.

With only the slightest hesitation, she accepted.

Chapter Four

"Did you buy your dress yet?"
Morty asked, surprising Sarah as she returned from her inspection of a lab.
Since the blackout, the systems had proved less than reliable, and physical inspection was now the rule, not the exception.

"Just a second, Morty. I've got to enter this security information into the computer." She turned to leave, but Morty knew she was only avoiding the issue and stood in her way. She sighed. "Okay, Morty, I didn't buy one yet."

He glared at her. "Then you'd better do it soon. My party's less than a week away."

"Don't worry, I'll get a dress." Sarah patted his arm reassuringly. "Besides, even if I don't, you wouldn't object if I came in my uniform, would you?"

Morty's mouth fell open. "Your uniform?" he

gasped. He had grown quite fond of her and wanted everyone he knew to meet and like her.

"I'm kidding," she said quickly, never thinking he'd actually believe her.

"Then why haven't you bought one?"

Sarah shrugged, although she knew full well it was because Ron, not Sin, was taking her to the party. Buying a dress would only be a confirmation of that fact. She was dreading going with Ron, but she had committed herself.

Since the electrical accident, she had seen Sin on a few occasions. Their conversation had been cordial but somewhat strained. Maybe it was her hopes interpreting reality, but every time they spoke it seemed as if he wanted to tell her something but was holding back.

"All right," Morty said, bringing her back to the present. "I won't bother you about the dress any more."

"And you won't say anything else about my going with Ron?"

"I—" he began, but couldn't go through with it. "I'll meet you at the front desk." He turned and left, pausing for a second to mumble hello to an older man who was wheeling a bucket with a mop down the corridor.

"What's wrong with Morty?" the man asked with a slight Irish accent. He was short and somewhat disheveled, with elflike features. It was as though a leprechaun had come to life.

"He doesn't understand," Sarah explained, although it wasn't much of an explanation.

"Who does?" the man asked, his eyes twinkling as if they held a secret. "The heart is a wonderful and mysterious thing. Morty's just stubborn, but he's not the problem."

Sarah looked at the man with wonder. "How do you know what my problem is? I think I would have remembered meeting you before."

"No, we've never met, but I know the look of someone having problems with love," he said with a sly grin. "Plus I don't go around with my eyes closed. I think I know what's going on."

"Then I wish you'd tell me." Sarah sighed.

"All right then, here goes." He leaned on the mop. "You've had a rough go of it recently, and, just when you thought things were looking up, you find they're no better than before. What you have to remember is that you're not the only one who's suffered a setback."

"Is this supposed to make me feel better?"

"No. You have to do that yourself. You have a situation here that you think you can't control. You want events to follow one path, yet they follow another. Now, I don't know how you can get what you want, but I do know you won't find out by sitting back and wishing. You have to go out and make things happen.''

Sarah found herself very much taken by what the man was saying, but many of her doubts remained. ''But what if things still don't turn out the way I want?'' she asked.

''Then you can't blame yourself for not trying. Sometimes you have to give fate a little kick in the pants, if you know what I mean.'' He winked at her and she smiled, feeling much better for having spoken with him. ''Oh, one last bit of advice: If there's one thing I've learned in all my years, it's not to read too much into matters. Freud himself said it best: 'Sometimes a cigar is just a cigar.' I hope that's helpful,'' he said. ''You're much too nice a person to be so unhappy.''

Sarah smiled. ''I feel better already,'' she assured him, and his eyes twinkled even more.

''I'm glad.'' He dragged the mop toward Pornaygun's lab. ''I'll be in here if you want to talk again.''

''Thanks.'' Sarah took a step away, then stopped and came back as she saw him open the lab's door. ''Uh, excuse me, but cleaners aren't allowed in there.''

''Quite right,'' he said and began to move into the lab. ''Have a good night.''

She grabbed the mop, which stopped his forward

progress. "You don't seem to understand. You can't go in there to clean."

The man looked puzzled. "But since cleaners aren't allowed in there, who do you think is going to clean it? Ron and Sin are fine lab assistants, but they're lousy housekeepers."

Sarah suddenly realized who the man was. "You wouldn't happen to be Dr. Pornaygun?"

"In the flesh." He winked at her again and pulled the mop and bucket into his lab. "It's been a pleasure speaking with you, Sarah. But you'll have to excuse me—there's a very messy lab I have to clean." He disappeared inside.

Well, she had always wanted to meet the mysterious Dr. Pornaygun. Sarah sighed and continued her rounds, finding nothing amiss.

Back at the command center, Morty was waiting with two other men. One was Johnny Douglass, the day security chief; the other person she didn't know.

"Sarah, this is Detective Tim Dover from the police department," Morty explained. She shook the man's hand. "You already know Johnny, who didn't have the courtesy to tell us about this meeting beforehand."

"I left you a memo a few days ago," Johnny stated calmly. "I can't help it if you don't check your mail."

"I look every day," Morty snapped, "and there's been nothing in my mailbox for the last week!"

"Shows how popular you are," Johnny mumbled.

"Gentlemen," Detective Dover interrupted, "you'll have plenty of time to fight later. Right now we're on my time, and I'd like to get started. Okay?"

Both Morty and Johnny nodded. Sarah knew there was no love lost between the two. When the decision had been made to keep the lab open twenty-four hours a day, Johnny, who had been Morty's assistant, lobbied the board to be named day chief. He did so by citing Morty's impending retirement and his own experience. Johnny campaigned hard, and the board eventually agreed with him. Morty, unaware of the ongoings, went to the board to suggest that Johnny be promoted. He was shocked and upset to hear what Johnny had done. The board, too, was disappointed, and, though the decision stood, Johnny was severely reprimanded.

Although she knew not to trust him, Sarah had always been cordial to Johnny. He seemed a bit aloof at times, but not nasty as he was with Morty.

Dover pulled a stack of papers from his briefcase and distributed a set to each of them. "Take a minute to look through these reports, and then I'll summarize the findings."

Sarah tried to read the technical jargon and began to feel a bit stupid. She glanced at Johnny and Morty, and was relieved to see that they, too, seemed to be having problems.

She put down the report and decided to take command of the situation. "What's the bottom line?" she asked.

Dover looked at her, then at the men. "The bottom line is that I don't think the transformer incident was an accident. We discovered small traces of explosives atop the transformer tower. We feel that the stolen car could have been placed there hours before the explosion."

Sarah was perplexed. "But why? No one stole anything from us or even tried to break in."

"Unless it was done for spite," Morty added. "New Idea has a lot of jealous competitors who would stop at nothing to sabotage us. Maybe they were trying to make it look like an accident."

Johnny tapped his fingers on the table. "We need to get all the facts before we start making accusations," he said. "Was anyone else serviced by that particular transformer? And how long a timer did the explosive have?"

"The power company confirmed that New Idea Labs is the primary power recipient on that line," Dover said, indicating the page that information was on. "We couldn't find the remains of the timer, but we do know the explosives that caused the accident are compatible with a long-term device, possibly as long as a whole day. We're still running tests, though. You'll be notified of the results.''

''I'll be your liaison,'' Johnny said, then added to Morty, ''That's a daytime job.''

''Go ahead,'' Morty responded to his baiting. ''I'm sure they won't be telling you anything we don't already know.''

Sarah ignored the bickering. ''So we know that the explosion was set deliberately, and, in all probability, with the purpose of crippling New Idea,'' she said, trying to bring the conversation back on track. ''Yet nothing was stolen. Do you think whoever did this knew that we have emergency generators and wouldn't lose anything?''

Morty snapped his fingers. ''Unless they weren't planning on doing something now—maybe they're laying the foundation for the future.''

''You're paranoid.'' Johnny dismissed Morty's theory and turned to Dover. ''Our security systems are famous for their effectiveness.''

''Maybe Morty is on to something,'' Sarah interrupted. ''Nothing seemed to be affected by the outage except the security systems, and those won't be fully operational for another few weeks.''

Johnny let out an exaggerated sigh. ''All you nighties are the same. If someone really had wanted to come in here, they would have set off a bigger charge at the power station, one large enough to really draw attention. Then they could have walked into an empty facility and taken whatever they wanted. That would have been the soundest strategy, if you believe your preposterous theory.''

''You're wrong, Johnny.'' Morty smiled as he spoke. ''Nobody could get in and out of New Idea without being seen. There's only one road leading here, and the transmission tower is on that road.''

Johnny saw he was wrong, but persisted anyway. ''What about by helicopter?''

''Too much noise,'' Morty countered. ''Anything like that would be spotted for miles.''

''I agree, but the point is moot,'' Dover said, cutting off their conversation. ''So the two theories are, one, it was a setup for some future scheme or, two, an attempt to sabotage experiments.''

''And, quite probably, an attempt to discourage other scientists from hooking up with New Idea,'' Johnny said, trying to make up for lost points. ''It all makes perfect sense.''

''Except for the timer,'' Sarah reminded him. ''What if—''

''I think it's pretty obvious they did that so they could get away,'' Johnny cut her off, looking at her as if she were brainless. ''They wanted to be long gone when that tower blew up.''

Sarah ignored him and went on, ''Or they may

have wanted to establish an alibi for what they were doing when it happened.''

Johnny began drumming his fingers again. ''Why would a saboteur need an alibi? He'd just do it, then get out.''

''Not if they're planning to come back,'' Sarah explained. ''In that case, they would want to have a good, solid alibi.''

''What kind of stupidity is that?'' Johnny snapped.

''No, it's a good thought—keep going,'' Dover said, and Johnny mumbled something to himself.

''Maybe the explosion was caused by someone who worked here and wasn't looking to break in,'' Sarah continued. ''Maybe they were looking for a way *out*.''

Chapter Five

The morning after the meeting with Johnny and Dover, Sarah still felt completely drained. They had discussed many theories, but each was found to have a flaw of some kind. She tried to put the whole thing out of her mind as she walked out into the sunshine and breathed in the crisp air.

It was earlier than usual. Morty had given her a few hours off so she could buy a dress, and the parking lot was still empty. She got into her car to find that the engine wouldn't turn over. She groaned and popped open the hood, but a quick inspection revealed that nothing was wrong. She went back inside, only to run into Ron.

"I know you're a dedicated employee," he said, "but you *are* allowed to go home every now and then."

"My car won't start," she told him.

Ron smiled broadly. "Consider your troubles over. I happen to be a terrific mechanic."

"Well. . . . If it's not a lot of trouble."

"It would be my pleasure." Ron took her arm and they went back to her car.

After ten minutes of tinkering and muttering, Ron gave up. "It's the strangest thing," he said as he closed the hood. "It won't start, but I can't find anything wrong."

Sarah sighed. "I'll call a garage. Thanks anyway, Ron."

"I wish I could have helped," Ron told her as they walked back to the labs, "especially after that rough meeting you had last night with Morty, Johnny, and that other fellow. Is there some problem at New Idea?"

Sarah opened her mouth to answer, then shut it. "Sorry," she said apologetically, "but I can't discuss it. It's a security matter."

"I understand." Ron's perpetual smile drooped slightly. "I didn't mean to pry—I was only wondering if I might be able to help. It's about that transformer incident, isn't it?"

"Well, yes and no," she said, and then stopped as they got to the front of the building. "I mean— no, we don't need any help, but I thank you for your good intentions."

"And the 'yes' part?"

Sarah knew she had said too much. "Yes, it was about the transformer, but I really would prefer that we drop the subject."

Ron looked sad again. "Of course. What's the matter with me? Here you tell me you don't want to talk about it, and I ask you another question." He hit the side of his head with his hand, then made a silly face.

Sarah laughed at him. "It's all right. I suppose we've all had a lot on our minds lately."

"True. Take our project, for example. We're getting to a crossroads point, and things are going well, but. . . . " He left the sentence unfinished.

Sarah was curious about what he was leading up to. "But what?"

"Oh, it's nothing," he said, then held up his hand before she could ask any questions. "Like you said, let's drop the subject. You've got your secrets, and I've got mine. Nature of the game, so to speak."

"I suppose," she said, her training and discipline stopping her from pressing further. "Well, thanks again for trying to help." She turned to go inside to call a mechanic, but Ron stopped her.

"After you make your call, why don't you leave your keys with Johnny and I'll drive you home? There's no sense waiting around for who knows how long."

"That's nice, but I need my car for some errands—''

''Say no more.'' He bowed to her. ''Ron's reliable cab service is at your command.''

Sarah looked around the lot. ''Your car isn't even here.''

''True,'' he said, ''but not for long,'' then pointed down the road where she saw it coming up the winding highway. ''Here comes that sinfully late fellow with our chariot.''

Sarah was somewhat surprised at what she found herself thinking. Stupid as it seemed, she didn't want Sin to see her and Ron leaving together.

''No thanks, Ron,'' she said, more firmly than before. ''I'd better stay here and make sure my car's okay.''

''Well, sure.'' Ron held his hands to his heart. ''But you've wounded me deeply.''

''You'll live.'' Sarah laughed and went back inside to find Johnny and Morty at the command center. Both men were reading Dover's report and making notes. Sarah told them what had happened, and each recommended a different repair service. Then they began to argue over the relative merits of their choice. Seeing the conversation heading for trouble, Sarah decided to call both services, saying she'd choose whoever could get to the labs the fastest. The repairman suggested by Johnny told her on the phone he'd be there within two hours.

Almost beside himself in his happiness over Sarah's selection, Johnny offered to hold her car keys and guide the mechanic in the right direction so she could go home. Morty began to grumble, and Sarah quickly went back outside, hoping Ron was still there. In her haste, she forgot all about Sin until she arrived at the car. Luckily, Ron was by himself.

"The mechanic won't be here for two hours. If you wouldn't mind giving me a ride home. . . . Oh!" She stopped, startled, as Sin stood up from the other side of the car. He looked at her strangely until he realized he had scared her.

"Sorry if I frightened you," he said. "I dropped my keys." He held them up for her to see.

"I wasn't frightened." Sarah wanted to say something else, but she didn't know what.

Sin put the keys away. "I'd better get to work." He took a briefcase from the car, his eyes not meeting hers. Sarah felt terrible, until a new voice rang out.

"Ron! So there you are, you scalawag!" the voice said, and Sarah turned to see Dr. Pornaygun walking toward them. "I said you could take a break, not the whole day off!"

Ron looked confused. "I thought we were finished," he protested.

"You thought wrong!" Pornaygun glared up at Ron. Although he was the least physically com-

manding of all four of them, he was still the domi-
nant one.

"Maybe I can take over," Sin put in. "Ron was
about to drive Sarah home—she has car trouble."

"You can take over, right after Ron and I finish
what we're working on," Pornaygun said to Sin.

Ron sighed. "Sorry, Sarah. Duty calls." He went
back into the lab and Sin made a move to go back to
his car.

"Where do you think you're going, Sin?" Pornaygun asked.

"To work," Sin said innocently.

"And leave Sarah here all by herself?" Pornaygun
looked as if he couldn't believe what he was hearing.
"Have you no compassion?"

"What about my work?" Sin protested, still not
looking at Sarah.

"You can do that right after you take Sarah wherever she wants to go," Pornaygun insisted. "Ron
and I should be finished with what we're doing by
then." Sin opened his mouth to protest, but Pornaygun continued, "I won't hear another word. Now,
off with the both of you."

Sin returned to his car. Sarah started to follow, but
Pornaygun motioned her over. "Make the most of
it," he whispered. "And when you get into town,
call the garage and tell them to forget it. Last night,
while you were all in that meeting, I snuck out and si-

phoned the gas from your car. I'll put it back by the time you come on duty tonight.''

Sarah's mouth fell open. No wonder they couldn't find anything wrong with the car! ''Why, you—''

''Don't thank me now—I'm only giving fate a little hand.'' He actually did a little jig as he left.

Sarah's emotions were mixed over what Pornaygun had done. On one hand, she felt awkward around Sin after she had accepted Ron's invitation; on the other hand, she was glad for this opportunity. Crazy as it seemed, she liked Sin, and, even crazier, she thought he felt the same way toward her.

''Perhaps you'd like to sit in the back and have me wear a chauffeur's cap?'' Sin asked as she entered the car. That burst her bubble in a hurry.

''This wasn't my idea, so don't get mad at me!'' she snapped. ''I'll call a cab since this seems to be too much of an imposition.''

She opened the door to leave, but he reached across and firmly but gently slammed it shut. She glared at him, but his eyes were full of sadness and her heart melted.

''I'm sorry,'' he apologized. ''I have a lot on my mind and I took it out on you.''

Sarah felt better. ''I have a lot on my mind too,'' she said.

Sin drove out of the lot and onto the road where the day workers were coming in. He had to drive carefully because of the traffic, giving them both the opportunity to cool down.

"Where would you like to go?" he asked after the majority of cars had passed.

"I have to go home and change out of my uniform. I'll take a cab from there to the mall to do some shopping." She didn't want to mention she was going to buy clothes for Morty's party.

"I hear you're going to the retirement party with Ron," he said suddenly, and Sarah tried hard not to blush. She phrased her answer very carefully.

"He was the only one who asked me," she responded, then turned bolder. "Are you going?"

"Yes." He kept his eyes on the road. "Morty doesn't seem to like me much, but Pornaygun wants me to be there."

Sarah took a deep breath. "Maybe you and your girlfriend can sit at our table," she found the courage to say.

"Girlfriend?" Sin looked bewildered.

"You know, the girl you were with the night of the transformer explosion." Sarah waited anxiously for his reply. It took a few seconds to come.

"Oh, her." Sin continued to look straight ahead as he spoke. "No, I won't be going with her."

"There's someone else, then?" Sarah marveled at her nerve in asking all these questions.

"I'll be at the party alone." His voice had a finality in it that stopped her from asking anything else. An uncomfortable silence settled in. He broke it as they passed the vandalized transformer. "Any more information on what happened there?"

Sarah's heart dropped and she felt terrible. "I'm sorry, but I can't discuss it." How typical. He was trying to make conversation, and it was the one subject she couldn't talk about.

"I understand," he said, and, unlike Ron, let it drop.

Sarah was determined to keep the conversation going, despite this setback. "I really was quite lucky you came along that night," she ventured.

"Maybe it was fate." This time he turned to face her. She gazed into his eyes and a warm feeling passed through her. It lasted long after he turned back to the road.

"Sin, where have you been . . ." she said dreamily, then caught herself. "I mean, where were you before New Idea?"

The corners of his mouth turned up in a small smile. "You're full of questions this morning."

"It comes with the job. My father used to tease me that I'd be a good detective one day," she said happily, then remembered the rest of it, "if only I'd been a boy."

"That must have hurt."

"A little, but it also inspired me to work harder to

make my dream come true. I had to. I did twice the work of anyone in order to make it on the police force.''

''That doesn't seem fair,'' he said. ''Everyone should be treated equally and given the same opportunity.''

Sarah's sigh echoed with the pain she had endured. ''Yes, but it didn't work like that. And since it was the only set of rules, that was the way I had to play.''

''How long were you a police officer?''

''Five years, until—'' Sarah stopped in midthought. ''Here we are talking all about me when you started to talk about you. I've been monopolizing the entire conversation.''

Sin laughed. ''That's okay. My life would only bore you.''

She smiled at him. ''I'm sure it wouldn't.''

''There's not much to tell. I was born—'' Sin suddenly stopped talking and jammed on the brakes.

''What's the matter?'' Sarah saw nothing wrong, but Sin was out of the car even before she had finished speaking.

He was looking down at something by the side of the road. Sarah saw it was a raccoon that had been hit by a car. The animal didn't seem to be able to use its back legs, and it was crying out in pain and fear.

''The poor thing.'' Sarah bent down to comfort it.

Sin knocked her hand away just as the raccoon snapped at her.

"Careful," he warned. "It's scared and doesn't understand that we want to help."

He returned to the car and pulled out a blanket and a pair of gloves from the trunk.

"We have to get this fellow some medical help, but he won't let me pick him up if he sees me coming," Sin said, as he put on the gloves and wrapped the blanket around his arms. "What I need you to do is stand in front of him and, on my cue, attract his attention. Then I'll grab him in the blanket."

Sarah looked into Sin's eyes. "That animal could have rabies." She was both scared and proud of what he planned.

"I hope not." He gave her the cue, and she did as instructed. Somehow he managed to scoop up the snapping, thrashing animal. He dove into the back of the car with the raccoon while Sarah jumped into the driver's seat.

"Drive!" Sin yelled as he wrestled with the animal. The squeals the raccoon let out were like shrieks in the close quarters of the car.

Sarah drove as fast as she possibly dared along the winding road and into town. To her horror, she realized she didn't know where to go. "Do you know any veterinarians?" she called to him.

"No!" Sin yelled back over the wailing. "Go to the hospital."

Sarah headed in that direction, and pulled into the emergency ward. She opened the back door, and Sin ran in with the struggling raccoon. A rather large nurse stopped them almost as soon as they entered.

"You can't bring that thing into this hospital!" she snapped.

"Yes, I can." Sin pinned her down with his eyes. "This raccoon is injured. This is a hospital, you're all supposed to save lives. Well, this is a life."

"It's not a human life," the nurse retorted, "and that noise is deafening! Get it out of here!"

"What do you propose we do with it?" Sarah asked angrily.

The nurse folded her arms. "I don't care what you do with it as long as you leave! You're disturbing the other patients!"

"Take the poor thing in," said an elderly woman who was sitting in the waiting room.

"I want to speak to a doctor," Sin said firmly. "You're not letting me in, I'm not leaving, and the raccoon is dying." The animal's thrashing had lessened, as had its mewling. Sin's arms, the blanket, and the floor were covered with blood. Sarah wondered whose it was—Sin's or the raccoon's.

"No," the nurse said stubbornly.

"Have a heart," Sarah pleaded, but the woman remained unmoved. Finally, a doctor came out.

"What's all the noise out here?" he demanded, and the situation was explained quickly. The doctor looked as sympathetic as the nurse had as he turned to Sin. "You do understand that this is not an animal hospital."

"I do," Sin said, "but I had no choice."

The doctor regarded Sin, Sarah, and the raccoon. "All right, bring it in," he said, and Sin followed him into the back. The nurse stopped Sarah from going after them, but she didn't protest.

One hour later, Sin returned, bandages covering his arms. Sarah ran to him, her heart pounding. "It's nothing," he said, anticipating her question, but it wasn't a good enough explanation.

"Nothing? You look like a mummy! What happened?"

"Barnum clawed through the blanket," he explained. "It's relatively superficial."

Sarah arched an eyebrow. "What exactly does 'relatively superficial' mean?"

"A few stitches, but basically it's only some cuts. Barnum wasn't rabid, so I don't have to worry about that."

"That's good." She was relieved he wasn't seriously injured. "Why do you keep calling him Barnum?"

Sin smiled in a silly way. ''I thought that instead of calling the raccoon 'it,' we might as well give him a name. I picked Barnum because P.T. Barnum was a showman, and that little animal sure did put on a show.''

Sarah laughed. ''How is our little showman?''

''He'll be fine, although he's lost a lot of blood. He'll have to be kept inside for a while. The smell of blood makes him a target to every creature out there,'' he said seriously, then a twinkle came back to his eyes. ''Not to worry though—the doctor says Barnum should be up and scavenging through garbage cans in no time at all.''

''And it's going to cost you an arm and a leg,'' the nurse bellowed as she stormed over to where they were standing. ''I don't understand why you didn't just leave it there.''

''I didn't think you would.'' Sin gave her a level look.

''You'll have to fill out these forms before you go,'' she said, thrusting a clipboard and pen at him. Sin held up his bandaged hands to show he couldn't. Sarah came to his rescue by grabbing the pen and board. The nurse left, and Sarah and Sin sat down to fill out the paperwork.

The forms contained a variety of questions relating to Sin's background, such as name, age, allergies, and childhood diseases. Though Sarah was sorry for the circumstances that brought them to this point, she was glad she could now find all this out without seeming nosy. Everything was rather dull until the question of whom to call in case of emergency came up.

"I don't know," Sin said after a long pause.

She was surprised. "You must have somebody you'd like notified. What about your family?"

"Not much of my family is left—only my father's sister, and she's getting on in years." Then his face lit up. "If it's not too much of an imposition, how about putting down your name?"

Sarah didn't know what to think. "Me?" was all she managed to say.

"Only if it's not a problem." His eyes held her gaze. "I'd really appreciate it. I know you can handle things in an emergency."

"That's very flattering, and—" she began, but the nurse came over at that moment and demanded the forms. Sarah didn't discuss the situation any further and put her name down on the paper, then handed the clipboard to the nurse. She turned to Sin. "Come on, I'll drive you home."

"But the project—"

". . . can wait," she finished his sentence. "I'll

call Dr. Pornaygun and explain everything. You need to go home and rest, and that's an order.''

''Yes, dear,'' Sin said with mock meekness. Sarah didn't care that he was kidding—she liked the sound of it.

Chapter Six

Because Sarah spent too much time daydreaming that it was Sin picking her up for Morty's retirement party, she found herself running late. She hurried to get back on track, but Ron came early, further disrupting her schedule.

"Don't you know never to pick a woman up early?" she scolded as she let him in.

"Take your time," he said, looking very dapper in his tuxedo. He sat down in her living room as though he had all the time in the world. "I don't mind waiting."

"I'll be ready in a few minutes." She went back into her bedroom, shut the door, and continued her preparations.

A few moments later Ron yelled, "Nice flowers," and Sarah groaned, remembering how she had meant to put the bouquet away. Sin had given them to her as thanks for her help in the hospital.

''Aren't they?'' she called back, but that didn't end it.

''From a secret admirer?'' Ron asked, and she could read nothing from the tone of his voice.

''No, nothing like that.'' She decided honesty was the best policy. ''Sin sent them to thank me for helping with the raccoon.''

Once again, Ron didn't let the topic drop. ''He's a strange one. Sin never fails to do the unexpected. Funny thing is, though, I've been working with him for quite some time now and I don't know much more about him than when we first met. It's almost as though—'' He stopped in midsentence as Sarah came through the door. He had never seen her out of uniform, and he was stunned at her appearance.

''What's the matter?'' she asked, feeling slightly uncomfortable. ''Is something wrong with what I'm wearing?'' She looked down at her black silk sheath dress, hoping it was appropriate.

''Sarah, you're beautiful!'' he exclaimed as he admired how the dress accentuated her lithe figure and how the makeup she seldom wore brought out the true beauty of her clear skin, brown eyes, and auburn hair.

''Thank you,'' she said, blushing. If only she felt about him the way she felt about Sin, things would be so easy. She sighed. Sometimes she wished she had never laid eyes on Sinclair Edwards.

Ron didn't move from where he had stood once she entered the room. "We'd better get going," she said, trying to coax him along.

"Right!" He broke out of his reverie and escorted her outside, where a huge white limousine waited.

"Only the best for the best!" He smiled broadly as he opened the door for her. Sarah thanked him and entered the car. Despite the fact she had always considered things like this to be self-indulgent, she was very impressed by the limo.

"It's wonderful," she said as she admired the interior. "But you really shouldn't have gone to all this expense."

"Think nothing of it." He inched closer. "What good is money if you don't use it?"

She smiled and moved away from him, but Ron followed. She moved again and was relieved when he eased up and went back to his own side.

"Care for a little bubbly?" He pressed a button, and a panel opened in front of them, revealing a champagne bottle on ice and two glasses.

"Maybe just one glass," she said, and it was filled even before her sentence was finished. After that, Sarah had to be careful because every time she took a sip, Ron topped off her glass.

They kept their conversation light as they were driven to the restaurant where the party was being held. She noticed they drove past the spot where Sin had found the injured raccoon.

"Isn't that where you and Sin had your close encounter with the raccoon?" Ron asked, echoing her thoughts.

Sarah nodded.

"That really must have been something," Ron continued. "I can imagine the faces of the hospital staff when you brought that creature in. Sin must be quite an animal lover."

"I suppose," Sarah said. "I really don't know that much about him."

Ron moved closer to her, but this time with a different attitude. "Neither do I, and that's been bothering me." His face became serious, and he put down his champagne. "You work with someone for a while, and you think you know them, but you really don't. I couldn't even tell you where Sin comes from. Do you know?"

"Sure, I. . . . " She didn't. "No, I don't know where he comes from, but then again, I don't know where you're from, either."

"That's easily remedied—I'm from Boston." He pronounced it with a New England accent. "And you?"

"New York, the Big Apple." She touched her voice with a trace of Brooklynese. "So you see, there's nothing mysterious. It just never came up in conversation.''

''That must be it,'' Ron said, and he settled back into his easygoing ways. ''He's probably one of those people who doesn't like to talk about personal things. Me, on the other hand. . . .'' The conversation changed to a light banter as he told tales of his M.I.T. schooldays all the way to the restaurant.

If Sarah was impressed by the limousine, she was stunned by the restaurant. It had a reputation for being one of the finest in the city, and it certainly lived up to its renown. From the moment they arrived at the neatly manicured grounds, there was opulence at every turn. Ron gave her his arm as they left the limo and she took it, hoping that anyone watching would recognize it for the harmless gesture it was.

They entered the fabulously decorated building and were escorted to the room where the party was being held. Although it was somewhat early, there was already a good crowd. Some of the people she recognized, but most she didn't, one of the disadvantages of working on a different shift.

''Hey, Ron!'' someone called, and Johnny Douglass strode over. His gait was somewhat awkward. Johnny slapped Ron on the back and gave Sarah a long, hard look. ''Ron, aren't you going to introduce me to your date?''

''Sure, Johnny, I'll be glad to introduce you.''

Ron was barely able to contain his amusement. "This is Betty."

"*Nice* to meet you," Johnny said. He leered at her, and then some sort of recognition dawned in his eyes. "Haven't I met you before?"

Ron spoke before Sarah could. "No, you've never met Betty, but we work with her cousin Sarah. There's a bit of a family resemblance."

Johnny hit himself on the forehead. "I see it now," he said, then started to laugh. "Only Betty's ten times better looking than that grim cousin of hers."

Sarah turned to Ron. "Don't you think this has gone far enough?" she asked, but he didn't even look at her.

"What's the matter, Johnny?" he baited the other man. "Don't you like Sarah?"

"Why, if I were the last man on Earth—" Johnny began, but Sarah didn't wait long enough to hear the rest of it. Seeing that Ron was not about to stop egging Johnny on, she turned and walked over to the bar. She ordered a club soda and sat dejectedly on a stool.

"Is that any way to act on such a happy day?" a voice from behind asked, and Dr. Pornaygun took the stool next to her. "You look positively lovely, Sarah, beautiful inside and out. Why, if I were forty years younger, I'd court you myself!"

She smiled, the doctor's considerable charm making her forget her troubles a bit. He saw right through her.

"What's wrong, Sarah?" he asked, concern spreading across his animated features. "I haven't had time to chat with you lately."

"Everything's going fine," she replied, then frowned as she saw Ron and Johnny still going at it. Pornaygun saw her expression and gave her a puzzled look. Sarah explained what had happened.

"That's sad." Pornaygun shook his head. "There comes a time when you have to start acting like a man. That goes for both of them. But enough about those two—I want to hear about you and Sin."

"Not much to tell." She took a sip of her soda.

"Well, there has to be something—I heard about you two and the beastie. Things certainly do happen when you and Sin get together."

She shrugged, and Pornaygun looked at her intently. "Remember what I told you about making the most of your opportunities," he said. "I don't know how much longer I can keep this up." He waved good-bye and moved off into the ever-expanding crowd.

There seemed to be people from every walk of life at the party. Sarah had never dreamed that Morty was so popular. Although she felt good that Morty's party was getting such a turnout, she was a bit apprehensive. After all, she was a stranger.

As she watched the faces come and go, a familiar one detached itself from the crowd and came toward her. Sarah's heart beat quicker. It was Sin, dressed in a well-tailored suit, and threading his way through the crowd with the agility of a cat.

"Hi," he said as he reached her. His expression was warm.

"Hello, Sin." Her heart was pounding at his nearness.

"What'll it be?" the bartender asked.

"A scotch and a club soda. And put an olive in the scotch please," Sin said, then returned his attention to Sarah. "Pornaygun likes olives."

"Oh, so you're getting the drink for him?" she asked, and he nodded. She looked into the crowd and saw Pornaygun watching them. The doctor quickly disappeared.

"Sarah? As long as we're alone, I'd—"

"Hello, Sarah!" Morty interrupted, and gave her a giant hug. "You look absolutely gorgeous. I'm sure Sin won't mind if I take you away from him. After all, it *is* my party." He grabbed her by the hand, but she resisted. She very much wanted to hear what Sin was about to say.

"Give me a minute," she pleaded, but Morty wouldn't take no for an answer.

"You wouldn't want me to be unhappy during my own party?" He looked at her with sad eyes, and Sarah turned to Sin with a "what can I do?" look.

"Go ahead," he said, looking a bit sad himself. "I'll catch up with you later."

"Good." Morty pulled her away before she could even say good-bye. Out of the corner of her eye, Sarah could see Pornaygun standing with arms folded, shaking his head in disappointment. She knew how he felt.

Sarah spent the next hour meeting everyone who had ever been a part of Morty's life at New Idea. It was very hard for her to compare the glowing picture they painted of him with her initial image. She realized how close the two of them had grown in the time they had worked together, and how sad she'd be not to have him around anymore.

When the whirlwind tour of Morty's life ended, she went back to the bar, both to get a drink and to see if she might be able to find Sin. Instead, she found Ron.

"There you are," he said, his perpetual smile on his face. "I've been looking all over for you."

She was still upset at his behavior from before.

"Why? Are you finished humiliating Johnny?"

"He doesn't need any help from me," he said with a laugh, but saw that she wasn't amused. "I'm sorry if that incident upset you. It's just that Johnny is such a self-important braggart that I wanted to do something to take him down a couple of pegs. You have to admit, he's not going to live down what he said tonight.''

Sarah thought about it and decided that she *was* sort of glad Johnny had been put in his place. ''You may be right,'' she admitted, ''but don't do anything like that again.''

''Anything you say,'' Ron replied and squeezed her hand. ''Now let's go sit down—they're going to be serving dinner soon.''

They turned to find Pornaygun blocking their way. ''What a fine couple,'' he said, and Sarah wondered what the doctor was up to this time.

''We do look good together, don't we?'' Ron beamed and struck a pose.

''Just like a picture,'' Pornaygun replied. ''Speaking of pictures, that's why I'm here. They're taking snapshots out in the lobby, and I wanted to get one of you and Sin for posterity's sake. I'd like to show everyone back home what handsome boys I work with.''

''Nice idea.'' Ron's smile threatened to take over his entire face.

''I knew I could count on you.'' Pornaygun gave Sarah another of his sly winks. ''Ron, you come with me, and Sarah, you go find Sin. We'll have this done in no time at all.''

Pornaygun and Ron left, and Sarah couldn't help but admire the doctor's imagination and determination. It almost seemed as if he wanted her and Sin to get together more than she did. She didn't know if his plan would succeed, but it was definitely worth trying.

She walked through the big crowd in a futile attempt to locate Sin. After a while, she gave up and decided to try a different tack. This time she stood still and observed the crowd, hoping that, if she couldn't find him, he might find her. A few moments of waiting brought nothing good—just Johnny Douglass.

"Lost your date?" he asked, laughing. He was drunker than before, and Sarah marveled that he could remain upright.

"I'm looking for Sinclair Edwards. Have you seen him?" She hoped that, even in his present state, he might be of help. It wasn't a good idea.

"Looking to play the field?" Johnny put his arm around her.

"No, thank you." She shook his arm off, but he put it back.

"Listen, Betty, I'm more of a man than both those lab boys put together." He dug his hand into her shoulder, as though that would prove it.

"Let go, Johnny!" she whispered fiercely, not wanting to cause a scene. He ignored her plea and pulled her closer. Sarah responded by applying pressure to a point on his arm that would hurt the most. In this case, his senses were so numb that it didn't matter at all. She was about to resort to more drastic measures when a figure intervened and pulled his hand off her.

"That's enough, Johnny." Sin's voice was threatening and his eyes smoldering, but Johnny wasn't taking the hint.

"Get out of my way, Edwards," Johnny warned, and he went into an exaggerated martial arts stance. "I'm a black belt, and I'll take you apart."

"Let it die," Sin warned.

"I'll let *you* die," Johnny grumbled, and he threw a punch that, despite his intoxication, flew hard and fast. Sin caught it in his hand with a resounding crash.

"Stop it!" Sin ordered, holding on to Johnny's fist. Johnny didn't listen and shot out a kick that Sin brushed aside with his free arm. Sin applied pressure to Johnny's hand and the man fell to his knees. "I'm going to let go now. Don't do anything stupid."

"All right, all right!" Tears were in Johnny's eyes as Sin let go. He stood up and rubbed his hand. "Quite a grip you have there." Then Johnny grabbed a glass of wine out of someone's hand and threw it in Sin's face. With a murderous roar, Johnny charged forward, only to be met by a thunderous punch.

Everyone in the place was gathered around, and Sin, his anger gone with the blow, looked very embarrassed. Ron, Dr. Pornaygun, and Morty all came to the front of the crowd.

"Was this really neccessary?" Morty asked as he bent down to inspect the dazed Johnny.

"I'm sorry I had to spoil your party," Sin said with his head down. He started to leave, but Sarah stopped him.

"Let him go, Sarah," Morty said angrily. "He's done enough damage for one night."

Sarah put her hands on her hips as she squared off with Morty. "If he goes, I go," she said stubbornly.

Ron's smile almost left his face. "Hey!" he cried. "What about me? I thought— Ow!" The rest of his statement was cut off as Pornaygun stepped on his foot on the way to help pick up Johnny.

By the time Johnny finally got to his feet, he had snapped out of his daze with a vengeance. "I want him arrested!" He looked around the crowd. "You all saw him attack me for no reason!"

Sarah was incredulous. "No reason?" she snapped. "He was only defending himself after you got mad when he stopped you from pawing me."

Morty whirled on Johnny, his bearlike frame shaking with barely controlled rage. "Is that true? You were rude to Sarah?"

"Sarah?" Johnny's mouth dropped open. "I thought . . . ."

"Can't we let bygones be— Ow!" Ron began, only to have his other foot stepped on by Pornaygun.

"Well?" Morty roared, his gaze shooting daggers at Johnny.

"She, uh, she came on to me," Johnny said, looking around for sympathy, but not finding it.

"Get out, Johnny!" Morty ordered, not wanting to hear any more. "Don't say another word—just go!"

Johnny stood up straight and tall, and dusted himself off in an attempt to regain some dignity. "I'll go, but don't think this is over between us." He glared at Sin and stormed out of the restaurant, knocking aside everyone in his way.

There was a long, silent pause and Sarah was scared that the party had been ruined. Pornaygun made sure that it wasn't. "Come on, everyone!" he called out. "Drinks are on me!"

A huge cheer rang out, and the crowd headed for the bar.

"I thought it was an open bar," Ron said as Pornaygun dragged him after the others.

"It is!" Pornaygun laughed, and soon Sin and Sarah found themselves alone.

"I didn't mean for all that to happen," he said.

"I know." Sarah put her hand on his arm. "It couldn't be helped."

"Sarah, I don't know how to say this, but I've wanted to. . . . " He was obviously groping for the right words. "You see, I'm so involved in my work, and I. . . . It's just that. . . . "

Sarah saw that he needed help. "Sin, are you trying to say that you feel the same way toward me that I feel toward you?" she ventured in a whisper. He responded by pulling her close and kissing her. She melted in his arms.

At the bar, Ron sighed as he saw what was going on. "Oh, well," he said.

"Don't worry, it's not a total loss," Pornaygun said, comforting him. "I've always wanted to ride in a limousine."

Chapter Seven

Sarah dreaded seeing Johnny that first day after the party. She imagined all sorts of scenarios, but it turned out to be nothing. Johnny simply gave her a terse rundown on a few minor problems, then left. He didn't mention anything about the night before, and Sarah said nothing about the dark black circle around his left eye.

No sooner had she sat down at the command center than the phone rang. It was Morty, making sure everything was all right and reassuring her that he could be there in twenty minutes if anything went wrong. She thanked him for his concern and promised to call if any help was needed.

After that, she took a deep breath and, before she could talk herself out of it, paged Ron. This was another scene she dreaded, but she had to talk with him. She traced his route to the command center using the surveillance cameras, and her heart pounded faster as he approached.

"Hi," he said, only the faintest trace of a smile on his face.

"About last night," she began, diving right into the matter. "I hope you'll forgive me for what happened between Sin and me. I didn't plan on it, and I want to apologize if you were hurt."

Ron laughed. "Don't worry. There are no hard feelings. Far from it, as a matter of fact. Sarah, I'd have to be blind not to see the way you and Sin feel about each other. I asked you to the party only because I knew Sin hadn't, and I thought that might get him moving. He's a bit slow about these things."

Sarah was surprised at Ron's explanation, but she was more than willing to accept it to keep things pleasant for all involved.

"I wish the two of you the best of luck, and I want you to know that I'm always here for you to talk to," Ron said. He extended his hand, but Sarah ignored it and kissed him on the cheek.

"I appreciate that," she said. Blushing a bit, Ron returned to his lab, leaving her with her thoughts. She was alone until three A.M., when Sin came out to join her. She was very happy to see him.

"When I took you home last night, you said I could see you again," he said, standing in front of the command center. "So here I am."

"So here you are," Sarah repeated. After he had dropped her off, she had spent the night dreaming about him. She felt like a teenager.

"It seems so funny," he said, and his gaze sent shivers through her. "I had been wanting to talk with you for so long, but one thing or another always seemed to get in the way. When I heard you were going to the party with Ron, I thought my chances were over."

"Sin, I went to the party with Ron because he asked me and I didn't want to go alone," she said, and thought this a good time to bring up a question she had pondered for some time now. "Besides, I thought you would bring that girl you were with on the night of the transformer accident."

Sin looked away. "Oh," he said simply.

"Oh?" She didn't feel very happy anymore.

He turned back to her. "I can see how you could get that impression, but she isn't a girlfriend—only an old colleague who happened to be passing through town." Sarah felt her depression end. "Sarah, I have to get back to the lab, but I wanted you to know I've been thinking about you, and that I'll be going out of town for a few days."

"Going out of town?" Her heart sank again.

"They don't need me in the lab right now, and I have to look in on my elderly aunt. I'll be back in two days, though, and I'd love to take you out then.

That would be Tuesday. How about I pick you up after work?''

''Sure, but that's eight A.M. Tuesday morning.''

''I know, and I have the perfect place to go,'' he said with a smile. ''Is it a date?''

Sarah smiled back. ''It's a date.''

On the morning of her date with Sin, Sarah came back from her last inspection to find Johnny unexpectedly at the command center. From the way he looked at her, she immediately knew something was wrong.

''Anything unusual happen on your last shift?'' he asked, confirming what she thought.

''No. Why?'' She could see he was trying very hard to hold in a smile.

''A little while after you left yesterday, I came to check on things. I made my rounds and found the door to the personnel office slightly ajar,'' he explained, still managing to hold in his smile. ''When the personnel director arrived, we went over the room and discovered the employee history files had been broken into. Nothing seemed to be gone, but the cabinet definitely had been tampered with.''

''Nothing happened while I was on duty,'' Sarah insisted. ''Something could have happened between the end of my shift and whenever you came in. Carl was on duty, and. . . . '' This time Johnny couldn't supress his grin.

"Carl? You mean Carl, the chairman of the board's nephew? Are you suggesting that the break-in occurred while *he* was on duty?''

Sarah groaned, knowing how the chairman adored his nephew. It could very well be the end of her job if she blamed him. Normally, she wouldn't hesitate to tell the truth, but she didn't want to risk losing her job. Besides, she couldn't be absolutely sure that the break-in hadn't happened on her shift.

She sighed. "I'll help with the investigation,'' she said, then remembered that Sin would be picking her up soon.

"No need.'' Johnny waved his hand, letting her off the hook. "I've got everything under control.''

"I still want to add my input,'' she insisted.

"Certainly. I'd let you do that now, but I know that this kind of thing must seem unimportant at the moment.'' Johnny pointed to one of the screens, which showed the parking lot. "Your boyfriend's here.''

Sarah saw Sin's car on the screen. "Leave your findings for me,'' she said as she picked up a gym bag packed with a change of clothes. "I'll check them over as soon as I get back on duty.''

Without waiting for Johnny's reply, she went to the ladies' room and changed into a T-shirt and jeans.

She came out to find Dr. Pornaygun and Ron standing near the exit.

"Taking a trip?" Pornaygun asked with a big smile.

"I'm not sure," Sarah replied. "Sin didn't tell me where we're going."

"I overheard him making plans, and I don't think you'll be disappointed," Ron put in, and Sarah was touched to see that he seemed genuinely glad for her happiness. They all went outside and met Sin.

"How was your time off?" Pornaygun asked him as he got out of the car.

"Fine. I got a lot accomplished," Sin said.

"Got a lot accomplished?" Ron repeated, looking puzzled. "I thought you were going to visit your aunt."

"I was and I did. I meant I got a lot accomplished for her." Sin opened the car door for Sarah. "If you'll excuse us, we've got a busy day ahead, and I'd like to beat the traffic."

"Of course," Pornaygun said. "Come on, Ron. I'll drive you home."

"Have fun," Ron called, and he and Pornaygun waved good-bye as Sin pulled away.

"How have you been, Sarah?" Sin asked.

"Good," she said, happy to see him again, but still upset at Johnny.

Sin picked up on it. "What's wrong?"

"Well . . . ." She thought about it and decided to tell him. "Johnny claims there was a break-in, except he has no evidence to prove it. I think he's trying to get even with us—I heard the board wasn't happy about his behavior at the party."

"What does he claim was broken into?"

"The personnel office, but, like I said, there's no proof."

Sin was lost in thought for a moment. "I think you should be careful around Johnny," he said. "At least until he gets over his anger."

"You're probably right." Sarah settled into the seat, feeling better about almost everything. "Sin, where are we going? I'm dying to know!"

"It's a surprise," he said, a mysterious smile on his face. "But I suggest you get some sleep. It's going to take us a while to get there, and you'll want to be fresh when we arrive."

Sarah was a bit tired, and decided to take his suggestion. She closed her eyes and within a few minutes was very contentedly asleep. All her dreams had to do with Sin and, after a particularly happy one, she felt herself being nudged awake.

"We're here," Sin said gently. "Did you have a nice nap?"

"Very." She looked around to see they were in a giant parking lot that was only about a third filled. "Where are we?" she asked, coming fully awake.

"Ever hear of Adventure Town?"

"You mean the amusement park? I haven't been to one in years!"

Sin's eyes danced. "Since it's midweek there shouldn't be a lot of people here. I hope this is okay with you."

"Okay? This is great!" she cried. "Let's go, and I want to go on every ride!"

"*Every* ride?" Sin asked with a groan.

"Yes!" She smiled, gave him a kiss on the cheek, and they were off.

The next two and a half hours passed in the blink of an eye. Sarah and Sin ran from ride to ride, only stopping when they were hungry. Racing each other, they ran to the refreshment area and bought all sorts of goodies, then sat down at a picnic table to enjoy their meal.

"What do you want to do next?" Sin asked as he devoured a hot dog. "I think we've covered all the rides."

Sarah smiled at him from behind her cotton candy. "Yes, but we haven't gone to the arcade or the circus!"

At that moment, a middle-aged man came over to them and slapped Sin on the back. "Josh, old buddy! Long time no see!" he said and sat down next to

Sin. "How have you been? I haven't seen you in, what is it, two years?"

Sarah looked at Sin curiously, and he returned her gaze with an equally puzzled expression. "Do I know you?" he asked the round-faced man.

"Do you *know* me? You are a kidder, Josh." The man slapped Sin again and laughed uproariously. Eventually, he calmed down and turned to Sarah. "Hi, I'm Robby Barton. Josh and I worked together at Dynamic Computers out on the Coast."

"Sarah Phillips," she said, and they shook hands.

"We're here visiting my wife's parents, and I thought I'd take the kids and escape for a while," Barton continued. "Confidentially, I think I wanted to come here more than the kids did. So, Josh, what have you been doing since the plant closed?"

"Mr. Barton," Sin began, "if you'll let—"

A little girl of about ten ran over. "Daddy, Mike stole my balloon and won't give it back!" she cried and then ran away.

"Kids!" Barton laughed and threw up his hands. "I'd better go before those two kill each other. It's been great seeing you again, Josh. Take care."

Barton gave Sin one last slap on the back, waved to Sarah, and jogged off in the direction his daughter had taken. Sin and Sarah looked at each other.

"Any idea what that was all about, Josh?" she asked with a giggle.

"Me?" Sin said in mock disbelief. "And all that time I thought he was talking about you!"

Sarah laughed, and the two of them finished their meal without further interruption. They moved on to the arcade area, where Sin challenged Sarah to a rifle game, and she beat him two out of three. That led to a succession of various games where they found themselves to be evenly matched. Somewhere along the line, Sin started to hold her hand. The day was going perfectly.

An announcement that the circus was about to start brought them out of the game room. They made their way to the circus tent and, on the way, ran into Barton again. He started to approach them, but his fighting kids took him off and running.

"Are you sure your name isn't really Josh?" Sarah asked as they took their seats in the small, one-ring circus tent.

"Of course it is. Sinclair Edwards is just an alias I used so I could get a job at New Idea and meet you."

"I thought so." Sarah laughed and hugged his arm tight.

The circus, though small, was very enjoyable. There were the obligatory clowns, a sword swallower, a lion act, and a fire-eater. Sarah tensed up slightly as the latter spewed out flames, but the act was over before it did more than stir the unpleasant memories. Sin didn't notice anything wrong with her, and her euphoria continued.

The dog act came next and Sarah laughed as she watched the trained canines go through their paces. She turned to see if Sin was enjoying it, but his head was turned away from the ring.

"Sin?"

"I'll be right back," he said, his voice tight.

"What's wrong?" she asked, but he was gone before the question was finished. After a few minutes had passed without his return, Sarah decided to follow. Once outside the circus tent she saw why he had left.

Stripped to the waist, he was using his shirt to put out a fire. The sword swallower and fire-eater were helping him, and they had managed to contain the blaze to a small grassy area. Clowns and workers were running over with buckets of water, and . . . . Suddenly, Sarah heard helicopters, and the world around her vanished, replaced by the nightmare rooftop scene.

Tears welled up in her eyes as she looked around and saw the apartment building fire snapping all around her. She heard screaming and saw the two children hanging on to a helicopter ladder. A gust of wind swept up and one of them fell to the rooftop.

"I'm coming!" Sarah yelled, but the roof in front of her was a fiery chasm between them. The helicopter came closer, its ladder dangling just out of reach over the flaming gulf. The child looked at Sarah, then at the ladder.

''Don't do it!'' she cried, but the child didn't listen. He jumped, grabbing the ladder with one skinny arm. ''Hold on!'' Her words couldn't give the child courage, and with a scream the boy let go and plummeted into the hungry fire below. His brother cried out and fell as well, bursting into flames as he hit the inferno. Sarah screamed out in agony and covered her face with her hands.

''Sarah! Sarah!'' a voice called out. With a heroic effort, she opened her tear-filled eyes to see Sin standing in front of her outside the circus tent. The fire had been put out, with only scorched earth to show it ever had existed.

''What's wrong?'' Sin asked, his face, red from the fire, showing deep concern.

''I don't know.'' She started to cry as he took her in his arms. ''I just don't know!''

Chapter Eight

"Sarah, the first step in curing a problem is admitting you have one," Sin said to her as she sat at the command center.

"I do not have a problem," she protested, her attention focused on the screens. "It was something that happened once and won't happen again."

Sin shook his head, walked away, then came back. Ever since the scene at the circus, Sarah had denied that it was anything but an isolated incident. She wouldn't talk about it and became very angry every time he mentioned it. That still didn't stop him from pressing her.

"I want to help you." He took her by the hand, but she pulled away.

"Then go back to Pornaygun's lab," she snapped. "If you'd finish whatever it is you're doing in there, maybe I could see you more. That would help me."

"If that's what you want," Sin snapped. He took a step away and turned back. She didn't look up, and with a sigh, he finally went away.

"There's nothing wrong with me," Sarah whispered to herself after he had gone. Even though she had said it hundreds of times since the circus fire, she knew it wasn't true. Further adding to her irritation was the fact that she couldn't put it out of her mind. Scared of what her dreams might bring, she also couldn't sleep. Even Morty's phone calls and Pornaygun's friendly greetings had done nothing to put her in a better mood.

Knowing it would irritate her more, but also realizing it had to be done, Sarah looked at the report Johnny had prepared on the break-in. All the report did was put blame on everyone but him, and Sarah began to write a scathing critique of what she thought of it. Her pencil broke in the middle of her frantic writing, and she threw it against the wall. She reread what she had written. The ferocity of it frightened her.

Sin came out of the hallway, where he had been watching, and put his arm around her. She looked up at him sadly and hugged him tight.

"I don't want this to happen again," she said, barely able to contain her agony. "I have to keep this job—I just have to!"

"Is that what this is all about?" he asked, stroking her hair. "No one's going to fire you."

"That's what the police department said, but that's not what happened." She fought to hold in her tears. "I lost everything then, and I don't think I could stand it a second time."

Sin lifted her chin so she could look in his eyes. "You'll never lose me," he promised softly. "We can beat this together."

"How would you know?" she asked, tensing.

"Because I had the same problem." He sat next to her. "Remember the story I told you about how I had saved two people from a lab fire?"

She nodded. "You said it was nothing."

"I was wrong."

"Then why didn't you tell me that before?" She looked at him accusingly.

"Because I didn't know how to tell it without looking like I was bragging. I think it's time I told you the real story. It might help."

Sarah sat back, hoping, yet doubting, that the man who had come to mean so much to her could help her.

"I was visiting a lab in Philadelphia when it happened," he began, his thoughts turning inward. "I had finished my tour of the facilities and was on my way out when I heard screaming coming from down the hall.

"I ran there as fast as I could and found a growing curtain of flames had trapped two workers against a wall. Quickly I found an extinguisher and yanked it off the wall, setting off the fire alarm in the process. With bells blaring all around me, and the antiquated sprinkler system putting out only a trickle of water, I used the extinguisher to open a passageway to them. Unfortunately, they were unconscious and I couldn't wait for help to arrive.

"As I later found out, volatile chemicals had mixed together, forming the fire and giving off toxic fumes. The fire contained the gasses until I started to extinguish the flames. Then the gasses escaped and hit like a wall, choking me. I staggered backward, ripping off my jacket and tying it over my mouth. I knew it wouldn't be enough, but I couldn't let those two people die.

"With a blast that emptied the extinguisher, I leaped past the sizzling wall of flames and picked up one of the unconscious men. I pulled him out of harm's way, then went back in for the other. Hoisting him up, I began the return trip out, but he regained consciousness and started coughing and thrashing. He slipped out of my grasp and fell into the fire. There was no other choice but to go after him."

Sin was breathing heavily, and Sarah was feeling her own experience licking at the corners of her mind. With a visible effort, Sin calmed himself and continued.

"He was on fire when I picked him up, so I carried him to a nearby portable shower. I pulled the handle, and a tidal wave of water washed over both of us and extinguished the flames. It was then that the first man I'd rescued returned to consciousness and told me there was a third man.

"Reluctantly, I went back. I found him completely engulfed in flames. I tried to reach him, but the fire was too fierce. I watched in horror as he burned, my only consolation being that he never regained consciousness.

"After that, help arrived and the three of us were taken to a burn unit. The two men I had saved were badly hurt, but managed to survive. The doctors marveled that I hadn't been burned severely. But I didn't feel lucky, not when I remembered the man I hadn't been able to save."

Tears welled up in Sin's eyes. "To this day I can see him burning, I can still smell . . . ." His voice trailed off and his fists clenched. Another few seconds passed before he could go on. "It took only a few weeks for my physical wounds to heal completely, but the mental ones lasted much, much longer.

"At times the memory of that day seemed like it would overwhelm me, but I kept on denying it. I pushed it into the back of my mind, until I finally snapped like you did at the circus.'' He stopped talking, obviously waiting for her to say something.

''What did you do then?'' she asked.

''I got help. But before I did, I had to admit I had a problem. That was the first step on my road to recovery.''

Sarah loved him for his frankness. It was as if she had known him all her life. She took a deep breath and did what she had to.

''I have a problem,'' she whispered, and felt better saying it. He took her hands and held her tight.

''Tell me what happened to you in the apartment-building fire,'' he said. She looked away for a second and he squeezed her hands tighter until her attention came back to him. ''Tell me, Sarah.'' He sat there patiently as, after a few false starts, the story came pouring out.

''What did your therapy consist of?'' he asked when she finished.

''Mental and physical exercises, day in and day out, until I was able to walk again and had the night-mares confined to situations of extreme stress.''

''And what about your pyrophobia? Did you tell them about that?''

''They knew about my nightmares.''

Sin looked at her sternly. ''I'm not talking about

the nightmares, I'm talking about your fear of fire. Why do you think you're scared of it?"

"Because it almost killed me."

He shook his head. "No. You came close to the real reason before."

Suddenly, Sarah tied everything together. "I'm scared of fire not because of what it is, but because of what it represents. It caused me to lose the thing I had worked my whole life for and, every time I see it, it reminds me of my failure and how powerless I was."

Sin sat and stared at her, and she grew a bit annoyed. "Well?" she asked. "What else do you want?"

"It's not what *I* want," he said softly.

"Then it must be what I want," she said, and he nodded. She sighed. From the bottom of her heart, she meant what she said next: "Sin, I need help."

He broke into a smile. "You got it!"

"I had to pull a lot of strings to get us in here, but I think it'll be worth it," Sin said a few days later as they walked up to the brick building in the middle of the fire academy grounds. "I think you're ready for this."

"Me too," Sarah said, hoping her shaking hands didn't betray her nervousness.

"It's all right to be apprehensive." He hugged

her. She appreciated the gesture, but it did little to reassure her.

"I'm not apprehensive at all," she said, looking into his eyes. "I'm scared."

"We don't have to go through with this if you don't think you're ready," he reminded her.

"No, you're right. The only way I'm going to beat this phobia is if I confront it." She pointed to the small building. "When do we go in?"

"As soon as Captain Vincent gets here," Sin said, then pointed to a figure walking toward them. "There he is now."

A man with a mustache, wearing a fire department uniform, strode up to them. "Are you Sinclair Lewis?" he asked.

"No, I'm Sinclair Edwards," Sin responded. "Sinclair Lewis was a writer."

"Nice to meet you, Sinclair," the fireman said, and the two shook hands. "I'm Captain Jim Vincent of the fire department."

"I'm Sarah Phillips," Sarah introduced herself.

"I hear you've got a problem with fire." The captain looked her over. "Well, don't worry about it anymore. After today you'll see how easily fire can be controlled and that there's nothing to fear from it."

"I hope so," she said, unconvinced.

"You will," Captain Vincent said firmly. "Now,

if you'll give me a few minutes, I'll see to the final preparations.'' He marched into the building and Sarah looked at Sin.

''How did you manage to pull this off?'' she asked.

He smiled. ''A friend called a friend who called a friend. It took a bit of doing, but, as I said, it should be worth it. When I had my fear of fire, this is what did the trick for me.'' Sarah gave him a puzzled look. ''What's the matter?''

''I guess I didn't realize when you told me your story that you had pyrophobia too.''

''Of course,'' he admitted. ''How do you think I know so much about it?''

Further discussion was cut off when the captain returned with two recruits. All three carried full fire gear. The recruits distributed a set to Sarah and Sin, then helped them into it.

''Thanks, boys.'' The captain nodded to the recruits and they left. He turned to face Sarah. ''I don't know how much Lewis has told you about what we're going to do, so I'll run over a few of the basics.''

Sin sighed, knowing it was useless to keep repeating that his name wasn't Sinclair Lewis, and looked to see if Sarah found it amusing. But her attention was focused on the captain.

''What you're going to experience in that building is what we call a 'controlled' fire,'' Captain Vincent, speaking in official tones, continued. "The building, in fact, is actually a long, deep room. In the back we're going to burn a wooden pallet. You with me so far?"

"So far, so good," Sarah answered, her heart beginning to race.

"There are three stages of fire," the captain went on. "The first occurs when the fire originates, the second happens when it burns, and the third is when it burns itself out.

"This is what's going to happen: The fire will light up the room, giving off sparks and smoke. As the smoke fills the top of the room, it'll begin to sink and we'll have to keep low, until we're on the floor. Also, the superheated gasses caused by the fire will make the temperature rise tremendously. It'll be roughly one hundred and ten degrees on the floor and two hundred degrees hotter toward the ceiling.

"Don't worry though, folks. This is a controlled fire and you're wearing full firefighter's gear, the same kind we use every day. It might be uncomfortable, but it'll be safe." He looked at them for acknowledgment.

"All right," Sarah said, trying to think about anything else other than what they were about to do.

They went to the door of the building, where the captain put on his gear and made sure theirs was working.

"Just breathe normally," he ordered, then turned on the oxygen supply. "Remember, if you have something to say, don't be afraid to say it."

Sarah found it easy to breathe in the helmet, and that comforted her somewhat. Captain Vincent opened the door and went in, with Sarah behind him and Sin bringing up the rear. When the door snapped shut behind them and the darkness surrounded her, all her comfort ended.

"Come over here." The captain's voice was tinny as it came through the helmet. They held hands and moved to the middle of the room. "You see that glow? That's the burning pallet." Off in the distance, it gave off sparks and smoke.

Sarah squeezed Sin's arm. This wasn't so bad. There was no reason to be afraid. With each passing moment, she felt her confidence growing.

"Look up," the captain ordered, and they did. There was an eerie orange glow near the ceiling. Smoke was swirling about and, like a dark portent, it began to sink lower.

"On your hands and knees," the captain snapped, and they dropped to the ground. "Listen carefully, then do exactly what I tell you. At my signal, I want you to take off one glove and raise your hand, but don't hold it there for more than a second. I only want you to feel the heat coming down. All right, go ahead."

Sin and Sarah did as they were told, and they found the temperature rose virtually every inch they lifted up their hands.

"Now, we're going to crawl out," the captain said, and he led them to the door. When they were outside, Sarah was actually disappointed that it was over.

"That's it?" she asked, looking from one man to the other.

"That's all a fire is," Captain Vincent said as he collected the equipment. "Nothing more than gas and flames."

"Disappointed?" Sin asked when the captain left to put away the gear. Sarah shook her head. "You shouldn't be. What you did was confront your fears and realize that they really weren't all that bad."

"I suppose," she said with a sigh. "But I thought it would be something more. I don't feel I've accomplished anything. I feel pretty much the same."

"Sarah, the problem's not physical, it's in your head," Sin told her.

"So when will I see a change?"

He shrugged. "Each case is different. When I went through this, my dreams started to lessen almost immediately. I hope you see the same results."

"So do I," Sarah whispered.

Captain Vincent came back and shook their hands. "I hope I've been of some help," he said, then pulled out a cigarette lighter. ''Remember, fire is your friend.''

The captain held the lighter flame toward them, and Sarah tried not to look upset when she felt a shiver run through her. She hoped it was only an involuntary reaction, and she didn't tell Sin about it.

That night, Sarah had the fire dream again. Only this time, she rescued the children. That she *did* tell Sin.

Chapter Nine

Sarah walked up to the front entrance of New Idea and put her identification card into the slot. It popped right back out, with the liquid-crystal screen displaying the words, *Access Denied*. She tried it again, and the same thing happened. A third time brought the same results.

She grumbled to herself and used the intercom to call the command center where she knew Johnny was on duty. She waved to the hidden camera and the door buzzed, unlocking the dead bolt. As she went to open it, the bolt reengaged and the door would not budge. All right, maybe it was an accident. She pressed the intercom once more, and once more the buzzer sounded. This time it stopped before her hand even got to the door handle.

"This isn't funny!" she yelled into the intercom. "I'm warning you, Johnny, I—"

A loud buzzing interrupted her, and this time it allowed her access, buzzing a rhythmic beat even after she entered. She stormed over to the command center to find Johnny turned around in the chair. Only his shoulders and the top of his head were visible.

"Listen, Johnny," she said, trying hard to control her anger. "I enjoy a joke as much as—"

"Who are you calling 'Johnny'?" the man asked, and turned toward her. It was Ron.

Startled, Sarah took a step back. "What are you doing here?" she asked, shocked.

"I've been holding down the fort waiting for you to arrive," he said, and jumped to attention. "Corporal Ronald Dancer requests permission to be relieved from duty, ma'am."

"Where's Johnny?"

Ron sat back down, then motioned Sarah over to look at one of the screens, which revealed Johnny, lying facedown on one of the couches in the lounge.

"Here's Johnny," he said gleefully. "Watch this." Using the override controls, he turned the lights on and off in the lounge.

"Ron!" Sarah slapped his arm. He ignored her.

"How are you feeling, Johnny?" he called over the intercom system.

"Not too good." Johnny groaned as he looked at the camera. His face was white.

"Well, don't worry. Soon you'll be as good as

new, and we'll be able to go out and eat pizza, and fried chicken, and hamburgers, and . . . ." Ron stopped as he saw Johnny get up and run for the bathroom. Chuckling, Ron switched the cameras to the bathroom, but Sarah turned off the screen.

"You're sick!" She turned to face him angrily.

"Me?" he replied, trying to look innocent. "I'm not the one who's sick. Your colleague in the bathroom, *he's* sick."

Sarah sighed, knowing Ron was in one of his moods. "Ron, get up and tell me what's going on."

With a flourish, he gave her the command seat. "Johnny and I went out to dinner, and I'm afraid what he ate didn't exactly sit well with him," he explained, still maintaining his innocent look. "I brought him back here where Carl was on duty, but Carl had a date and didn't want to stay late. It's nice to be of royal blood, isn't it?"

Sarah looked at Ron. "So you took over for him?" she asked.

"So the extremely important task of manning this vital nerve center fell to Corporal Ron Dancer." He jumped to attention again. "I'm happy to report that, besides the man throwing up in the bathroom, everything is okeydokey!"

"Thank you, Ron," Sarah said, and despite his teasing, she was glad he had taken control of the situation. "Is there anything you've done around here that I should be aware of?"

He thought for a second. "Would that be counting or not counting the small nuclear device I set to—"

"Ron! So there you are!" Dr. Pornaygun strode up to them and glared at his assistant. "You said you were going out for a quick bite! What did you have, two hundred courses?"

Ron's innocent look changed to an apologetic one. "Sorry about that, Dr. P. I tried to call in, but you didn't answer. Since I know how you get absorbed in your work, I didn't keep trying."

Pornaygun frowned. "I don't recall the phone ringing, but you're right, you rascal, I can't honestly say it didn't. What were you doing, anyway?"

"I had to take over for Johnny."

"Ronald Dancer," Pornaygun said sternly, "what have you done to him now?"

"Nothing. He got sick from something he ate."

"And I'm sure you had nothing to do with that," Pornaygun said, and Ron could barely suppress his smile. "Well, I can't do anything about the past, but the present is mine. Get back to the lab, and make it snappy!"

Ron hurried off, leaving Pornaygun and Sarah to stand there looking serious.

"I suppose Johnny did have it coming," Pornaygun said and began to laugh. "Ron really knows how to tell a good story, doesn't he?"

"That he does," she answered.

"So, how have you been, Sarah?" He cradled her hand in both of his. "I apologize for keeping Sin away from you, but we're at a critical point in our experiment. If anything's going to happen, it's going to happen soon."

"It must be exciting." She wanted to ask him, as she had wanted to ask Sin, what was going on in their lab these last few active days. Her professionalism was stronger than her curiosity, though, so she said nothing.

"It's very exciting, but very dangerous." For the first time since she met him, he was totally serious. "If you ever hear an alarm go off, get everyone, especially yourself, out of here as fast as possible. I can't say anything else, but remember what I've just told you."

"All right." His tone put her on edge. "Is there anything I can do to—"

"No. I don't expect there will be any trouble, but I appreciate your concern," Pornaygun said with a smile.

"I'm here if you need me." She smiled back.

"You're a comfort. When this whole thing's over, I'm going to take you out for the grandest dinner you've ever had!" Pornaygun promised. Then his eyes turned to the screen and he switched on the lounge intercom. Johnny, white as snow, had returned.

"We'll have a veritable feast, we will!" Pornaygun called into the intercom with much glee. "There'll be thick juicy steaks, and greasy French fries, and a slab of gooey pie that will—"

Johnny groaned twice, threw his hand to his mouth, and ran for the bathroom again.

"Dr. Pornaygun!" Sarah couldn't believe what he had done.

"All in a night's work," he replied, and waved to her as he went back to his lab.

Sarah smiled as she sat alone. She thought of how lucky she was, how well she had rebuilt her life after the fire that had cost her the police job. The injury she once had regarded as a curse was now hardly noticeable, and somewhat of a welcome reminder of how far she had come.

While her career at New Idea was not as exciting as her job on the force, it was still a challenge and a major responsibility. She took it seriously, and was even working on some innovations that would better safeguard the facility and save money in the process.

She also realized how much she had been missing all these years: In the police department, she had risked her life for her career; at New Idea, things were decidedly different. Even though she and

Johnny had their arguments, it was a friendly environment. Dr. Pornaygun was a good friend and really seemed to care about her. Morty was the same way, and they kept in touch on a regular basis. Ron, though a bit immature at times, was also a friend.

And then there was Sin, the main reason she was so happy. The handsome, quiet scientist made her feel good to be alive. Every second she spent with him, whether it was strolling hand in hand, or just having a conversation about nothing in particular, was magical. She had had a number of relationships with men in the past, but nothing like this. Sarah had never really believed she would find true love, but that was before she met Sin.

And the best part was that he felt the same way. It was enough to make the horrors of the past seem worthwhile.

At three in the morning, Sarah got a call from Morty. He claimed to be having trouble sleeping, but she knew he woke up on purpose to talk with her. Though she didn't like the fact he was ruining his sleep patterns to telephone her, she did enjoy their conversations.

"You're sure you've checked everything that I showed you?" Morty asked, going through his usual routine.

She sighed. "Yes, Morty. I've made a list, and I've checked it twice."

"Very funny. Now, what's going on between you and that Sinclair Edwards? Have you broken up with him yet?"

Sarah truly liked Morty, but this aspect of him very much annoyed her. She couldn't figure out why he disliked Sin, and he always skillfully avoided all her questions on the subject. This time she was determined to get some honest answers.

"Morty," she said, "you know how I feel about Sin. Why do you continue to hurt my feelings by saying things like that?"

There was a brief pause before he spoke. "I'm sorry. I don't mean to hurt you, Sarah. I won't do it again."

Usually, that was as far as the conversation got. But not this time—Sarah pressed him.

"Why do you dislike Sin so much?" she asked. "Is it that you don't like his type, or is it something else? Please tell me what's going on. Maybe this whole thing is only a misunderstanding."

"It's no misunderstanding." Morty's voice was low and grim. "Let's drop the subject. It won't do either of us any good."

Sarah gripped the phone hard. "No. I want to hear what it is," she said firmly. "Especially if it's something I have to know."

Again there was a long pause. "Suit yourself," he said finally. "As you know, Johnny claims there's been a break-in at the personnel office. It's not the first time that—''

"You don't think Sin is responsible?" Sarah broke in.

"Please, let me finish," Morty said. "I came to this job after twenty-five years in the Army. I retired as a lieutenant and decided to enjoy some time off. It's funny how things don't turn out the way you plan. Did I ever tell you that I was married?"

Sarah was a bit taken aback. "No, you didn't." In their time together, Morty had only mentioned his past briefly. The subject rarely came up.

"I met my wife overseas, and even though she was twenty years younger and pretty enough to have anyone she wanted, she wanted me," he said, his voice cracking with emotion.

"We were married two years, the two happiest of my life. I had just retired, and we were looking forward to our future together. A drunk driver cut all those plans short. How I wished it could have been me instead of her, but you can't change the past."

Sarah searched for words. "I'm sorry, Morty."

"Thank you, but I didn't mean to bring this up to be melancholy. I wanted you to know the background I brought to New Idea. Anyway, I didn't have any reason to stay retired, and I didn't want to be in the

Service again. Through my connections, I found out about New Idea Labs and was hired as security chief. I handled everything myself, until three years ago when Johnny came on board. He was actually a nice kid back then.

"In all my years here, I've seen a lot of people and security systems come and go. There have been some minor incidents, but nothing really serious until Pornaygun, Dancer, and Edwards arrived. I knew there would be problems as soon as I was denied access to their backgrounds.

"I raised a bit of a fuss about them and, to my surprise, so did Johnny, but it did no good. The best I got was an apology from the board and orders to keep a careful eye on that lab.

"From the moment they arrived, I made it my business to get to know the three of them. I found that Seamus Pornaygun was an honest, trustworthy man; the other two I wasn't sure about. Ron was the same as he is today. Some like that type, I guess, but I don't. Sin was always quiet, but in a suspicious kind of way."

"Like how?" Sarah butted in, trying as best as she could to remain neutral.

"He always avoided eye contact and purposely went out of his way to avoid social situations. Some people might call that behavior shyness. I call it suspicious. My background, I'm afraid, hasn't made me a trusting sort.

"On talking with Pornaygun, I found that he didn't know much about either of them. The pair had been assigned to him by the government and, since it provided the funding for his experiment, he never questioned the decision. As far as he was concerned, the two men were able scientists."

Morty sighed. "Shortly after they all arrived, I began to notice minor things wrong—misplaced files, doors left open, and things like that. Separately it meant nothing, but together it meant trouble.

"One day something odd happened. I was manning the command center routinely when suddenly the alarms in the west wing sounded and the camera went blank. Just before I lost the picture, I caught a glimpse of Sin coming toward that camera. I ran to investigate, and I found the lab next to Pornaygun's had been broken into, and files and drawers were strewn about.

"I confronted Sin and told him what I had seen. He claimed to have been on his way back from the bathroom when he heard a noise. He turned to see what it was and, he said, that's when I saw him. I didn't believe him, but I couldn't find any evidence to link him with the break-in, nor could the police."

"It could have happened the way he said," Sarah pointed out.

"No," Morty replied, "there were just too many coincidences for my taste, and I'm too good a judge of character not to know that there's something he's not telling."

"I see," Sarah said. Morty had been right, she thought. She was sorry she had pressed the conversation.

"But that's not going to stop you from seeing him, is it?" Morty asked. His question was greeted with silence, so he added, "No, forget I asked that. It's not fair to you."

"No, it isn't," she said, trying to sort out her thoughts and feelings. "I appreciate what you've told me, but it really is only circumstantial evidence. I do believe that *you* think he did it, though."

"Sarah, the last thing I want to do is hurt you, but you have to think more with your head than your heart."

"Morty, I don't—" Sarah stopped, suddenly noticing movement on the screen that showed the area outside the front door. Try as she might, she couldn't make out who or what it was. "I'll call you back," she said.

"What's wrong?" Morty asked, immediately catching the change in her voice.

"Probably nothing. I'll call you back."

"Sarah, tell—" Sarah hung up and stared at the screens. She went from camera to camera, but they

showed nothing. She couldn't dismiss it, though—
she was too thorough for that.

Her heart beating faster, she got up, took out her
nightstick, and went to one of the side doors so she
could sneak up on any intruder. Briefly she thought
about calling the police, but, by the time they arrived,
the incident would be well over. Besides, she
thought, she could do as good a job as any police
officer.

With very little noise, she slipped out the door
and moved through the hedges. Her heart raced even
faster, but from excitement rather than fear. She
knew this was dangerous, but it was the kind of
danger she felt comfortable with. It was what she
was born to do.

Suddenly, she saw movement up ahead. She
crouched down and advanced. As she did, the figure,
crouching too and breathing heavily, began to come
toward her through the shrubbery. Quickly, she took
out her flashlight and turned it on, holding it well to
her side as she played the beam around the bushes.

''Freeze!'' she roared as the figure leaped at her.
She sidestepped the oncoming form and was about
to bring her nightstick down upon it when her brain
registered what her eyes saw.

Her light was shining not on a man but on a Lab-
rador retriever. The dog was squinting into the light
and wagging his tail in delight. He came over and

rubbed up against her leg. Sarah bent down and scratched his head, her heartbeat returning to its regular pace. The dog licked her face and she laughed, releasing all her energy with the sound.

''What's the matter?'' she asked. A check of the animal showed no identification. ''Are you lost?''

The dog kept right on licking her. She saw he was reasonably well groomed, although a bit mangy, as if he had come a long way. She surmised that the dog had gotten lost and somehow made his way up to New Idea.

Sarah glanced around to see if there was anyone around who might be looking for the animal. She saw no one. Patting the dog on the head, she told him to follow her. Maybe the police had a report on a lost dog. In the meantime, she'd take him inside and give him something to eat and drink.

The dog followed her willingly, and they were almost at the front entrance when the lights snapped off. A few seconds later, the emergency generator kicked on and the eerie red emergency lights came to life.

Leaving the dog, Sarah sprinted to the front doors, only to find them locked. Through the smoky glass, she could see a shape at the command center. She pounded on the door, and the figure ran away.

Sarah pulled out her emergency override card. That didn't work and neither did a more conventional key. Anxiety flooding into her, she tried to yank the door off its hinges, but it was too sturdy.

She ripped off her jacket and wrapped it around the arm that wielded the nightstick. Tucking her head in, she swung the stick with all her might, producing a weblike pattern of cracks on the dense glass. She tried it again, and this time heard a resounding smash as the glass shattered inward.

She punched out the remaining shards with her jacketed hand, then clambered through the opening she had created. She ran to the command center and phoned the police. Unsure of what was happening, she knew it wasn't fair to the people at New Idea if she didn't call in outside help. It was what she should have done in the first place.

The police told Sarah to stay put and wait for them. But she couldn't just sit there. It was her job to provide security for New Idea. Until help arrived, that was exactly what she was going to do.

Sarah switched the surveillance screen back on and was thankful when it flickered to life. She switched from one camera to the next, trying to get a fix on where the intruder was. Finally, she located a shadowy figure in the semidark lounge. The only people in the labs tonight were Dr. Pornaygun, Ron, and . . . Johnny! Johnny was sick and in the lounge with the intruder!

Her head throbbing and her leg starting to hurt,

Sarah hurried to the lounge. The electric door opener was disabled, but she could gain access by changing it to the manual mode. She did so, and not wanting to present an easy target, tumbled into the room.

Springing to her feet, Sarah turned on her flashlight and played it around the room. The light revealed nothing but Johnny, who was still lying semiconscious on one of the couches. She took a step toward him, and suddenly saw a blur of motion out of the corner of her eye.

Sarah whirled to face the intruder and something flew through the air. The object hit her arm, not doing any physical harm, but it knocked the flashlight from her hand. She didn't bother to retrieve it, grasping instead her nightstick in a tight, two-fisted hold. She stayed silent, waiting for a sound to betray the intruder's location. But Johnny's heavy breathing made it impossible.

Remaining as calm as possible, Sarah picked up a nearby ashtray and flung it a few feet to her right. As she did, the figure moved and Sarah jumped after it, bringing the nightstick around in a low, sweeping motion. The intruder must have seen the blow coming and sidestepped. Whirling about in a kick, the figure hit her gently, but heavily enough to fling the stick away. The person then moved quickly toward the exit, but Sarah leaped to intercept. Her leg hurt, but she could live with the pain, at least for a while longer.

"There's no way out of here," she said. Her eyes were somewhat accustomed to the dim light and she could see that the intruder was burly, undeniably male, and strong. He made several feints to get by her, but she stood her ground.

"The police will be here soon," she warned. "You'd be better off giving up before they arrive."

"No," the intruder mumbled. Sarah prepared herself for an attack as his hand reached into a pocket. She saw the glint of light on metal and wished she had waited for the police. She had no defense against a gun.

"Don't do anything stupid," she said, hoping the intruder might listen to her.

"I won't," he mumbled again, and she heard a clicking noise. There was a flash, and she braced for the impact, but nothing came. The sound she heard, the light on metal she had seen, was not a gun . . . it was a cigarette lighter.

"Look at the flame!" the intruder ordered, and Sarah felt more fear than when she thought he held a gun. The dancing fire took all her interest, and no matter how hard she tried, she couldn't take her eyes from it.

Then the images began to return. "I'm cured! I'm cured!" she cried. But her protestations did no good.

As if magically transported, she found herself back in the burning apartment building where the two children were smiling evilly at her.

"Stay with us," one said.

"Forever!" the other added, and the two of them came toward her, their hands bursting into flames.

Sarah backed up until she was at the edge of the building. The ground was far below her, and the children, now completely inflamed, kept coming closer.

"Stop!" Sarah yelled, but they kept on coming and she could feel. . . .

"Sarah! Sarah!" a voice called, and she felt a stinging sensation. The world of the apartment building faded, to be replaced by Dr. Pornaygun standing in front of her. She was back in the lounge and there was no sign of the intruder.

"Are you all right?" he asked, his face lined with worry.

"No, I'm not," she said, and tears streaming from her eyes, she collapsed into his arms. "Not at all."

Chapter Ten

Sin put down his newspaper and stood up to meet Sarah as she came out of the psychologist's office. "So?" he asked. "What did she say?"

"What we already knew." Sarah sighed. "I have to face my fears in order to conquer them. She told me I'm still not confident enough to put this thing behind me. That's what's causing the problems."

"That's preposterous." Sin took her hands in his. "You're one of the strongest people I've ever met. I've got a good mind to go in there and tell her what I think about her prognosis!"

Sarah took his arm and walked him out of the office before he could make good on his threat. "It's better that you don't talk to her. She wasn't too thrilled about your idea of taking me to the fire academy."

His face registered surprise. "But that treatment

worked for me. What kind of psychologist is she, anyway?''

Sarah shrugged. ''You tell me—you're the one who recommended her.''

''All right, so I don't agree with her on a few minor points. But that doesn't alter the fact you need help. Your problem isn't going to get any better by itself.''

''I didn't need this,'' Sarah said stubbornly. ''I could have handled this by myself.''

''You've been proved wrong every time you've said that,'' Sin reminded her.

As if by mutual consent, they let the subject drop. They left the building and went to the garage where Sin had parked. It was noon, and she had an hour before she was due at Detective Dover's office to give a report on the intruder. She and Sin decided to have lunch, and he drove to a nearby diner.

''Are you sure you feel up to this today?'' Sin asked after they had ordered. ''We can postpone—''

She held up a hand, stopping him. ''I can do this,'' she said.

''I know you can.'' He smiled at her, his eyes warm.

Sarah stirred her coffee. ''You know, it's interesting. That break-in wasn't the only thing that happened that night.''

"What else do you remember?"

"Right before it all happened, I got a phone call from Morty. It's funny, he and I worked together for months, yet there was so much about him I didn't know."

"Sometimes things don't come up in conversation," Sin said. "Do you find that unusual?"

"It wasn't that; it was something he said. Something that's kind of awkward to bring up."

His eyes searched hers. "What is it, Sarah?" he asked. "I guess that means it was about me."

"Well, yes. I pressed Morty about why he didn't like you, and he told me—"

Sin took over the conversation. "He told you about the break-in he thinks I was responsible for. Don't feel awkward about it. The whole thing was just a misunderstanding that Morty can't accept."

"So what happened?" Sarah pushed on, hoping that it would turn out to be a simple mistake. She couldn't bear the thought of what might happen if it was otherwise.

Sin laughed. "It's all very simple. When I came to New Idea, there were a number of break-ins— well, not really break-ins, more like petty thefts. Anyway, Morty didn't get along with Ron and me right from the start. Ron came on too strong and rubbed him the wrong way, while I was a little shy and too much of a loner for his tastes. When he added our classified backgrounds to that, Morty found us very suspicious. I can't say I blame him.

"The night in question, I was on my way back from the bathroom when I heard a noise. I followed the sound to a camera that had wires hanging down and was starting to spark. I went back to my lab to call Morty, but he was already on his way to investigate. Naturally, his dislike for me, coupled with the circumstantial evidence, made me his prime suspect. I was vindicated by everyone but him, and though I've tried to make up for it, I've never been able to.''

Sarah watched him carefully as he spoke, and she believed him. "I knew it had to be something like that,'' she said with a smile, then looked at her watch. "It's getting late.''

Sin paid the bill and they left the restaurant. When they reached his car, he put his hands on her shoulders.

"It won't be long before our experiment is over,'' he said, gazing into her eyes. "When that happens, I'll have to move on to my next assignment, wherever that may be.''

Her heart sank. "Are you saying good-bye?''

He shook his head, frowning. "Of course not.''

"Then what are you saying?''

"I'm saying that even though I might not be working at New Idea, I don't want to lose what we've found.''

''I feel the same way, Sin, but we might have a problem.'' She spoke frankly, hating everything she had to say. ''I don't want to give up my career here.''

''I know.'' He looked at the ground. ''It wouldn't be fair of me to ask you to.''

Sarah felt terrible. ''Then we do have a problem.''

''Hopefully not. I thought you might say that, so I've asked to be assigned here permanently. I haven't heard whether they've accepted my application, so. . . . '' He shrugged. ''I just wanted to know if our feelings were mutual.''

She took his hands in hers and their eyes met. ''Couldn't you tell?''

His smile lit up his face, and he pulled her close. Their kiss was warm and tender, and Sarah wanted to stay in his arms forever. Then his watch alarm went off.

He sighed and pulled away. ''There's all the time in the world for us, but your meeting won't wait.''

''I know—darn it.'' She sighed too, and climbed into his car.

A wave of nostalgia swept over Sarah when she entered the police station a few minutes later. She stood and looked around, drinking in the atmosphere she knew so well and missed so much.

"Can I help you?" a tough-looking desk sergeant asked.

"Yes," she replied. "I'm looking for Detective Dover's office. I'm from New Idea Labs."

"Down there." The sergeant pointed out the way. She walked down a hallway to a door that read *Detectives*.

The room was small and smoky, but Sarah didn't mind. It was like coming home again. No matter what she was here for, it felt good to be back.

Sitting around a table in the room were Johnny, Morty, and Dover. Sarah was a little surprised to see Morty, but figured that they probably wanted his expertise.

"Hello, Sarah," Morty said as she came in. Johnny nodded at her as he lazily finished a cigarette, and Dover indicated the remaining empty seat at the table. She sat down.

"Let's get this started," Dover said. "We've already gone over most of this, but we have to run through it again. I want some answers, and I want them now. Morty has drawn up a list of things that have happened over the past months. I'd like to get your input."

Morty handed out copies of his report to Sarah and Johnny. Johnny made a face, obviously resenting that Morty was still in charge, but he said nothing.

"What's happened is a number of minor incidents

interspersed with a few major ones,'' Morty explained, paraphrasing his report. ''From the suspected missing files to this latest break-in, it's obvious that someone is trying to get something from us, and they're doing it one piece at a time. I just don't know what they're after.''

''That's not hard to figure out,'' Johnny put in. ''New Idea is well known for both its equipment and its secrets. Whoever is responsible for this wants one, if not both.''

''But why do it this way?'' Sarah asked. ''Why not do it in one strike instead of these little incidents that are sure to put us on guard?''

''Whoever's doing this has to know that everyone's on alert,'' Dover said. ''That's what makes it so hard to figure out.''

''Unless he's not all that smart,'' Johnny said, lighting a match for another cigarette.

Morty blew out the match as it burst into flames, saying, ''One's enough.'' Johnny grumbled but didn't try to light another.

''All right, let's forget about a motive for the moment,'' Dover said. ''What about suspects?''

''I've got one.'' Morty turned to Sarah. ''I'm sorry, but I think Sin is our primary suspect.''

Sarah felt as if she'd been hit with a hammer. ''Present your evidence,'' she said, trying not to show her dismay.

"You all know I saw Sin fooling around with the camera during that first break-in," Morty reminded them. "I know he was found innocent of that, but he was also there when the car accident happened and—"

"He said he was with a friend that night and heard the explosion," Sarah interrupted. "Then he came to investigate."

"Who was that friend?" Johnny asked.

Sarah shrugged. "We never asked. I'm sure Sin will tell us if we do."

"We will," Dover said, then nodded to Morty to resume.

"I think this third incident is the most damaging of all," Morty continued. "Up until that point, no one knew about Sarah's pyrophobia except me . . . and Sin."

"Pyrophobia? Really?" Johnny's face lit up and his hand reached for the matches. Morty was quicker and snatched them away.

"The thief used fire to escape from Sarah, which is something that Sin would do if he wanted to avoid hurting her physically," Morty went on. This statement hit Sarah like a clap of thunder.

"Wait a minute," Johnny said, groaning. "I'd like to hang Sin too, but we have to remember the personnel files that were broken into. Anybody who took them would have known about Sarah's accident

and deduced that she was afraid of fire. I'm surprised
I didn't realize it myself."

Is it that obvious? Sarah wondered.

"You're also forgetting that Edwards had access
to any file in the lab," Dover pointed out. "Why
would he have to sneak around if he could walk right
in and take whatever he wanted?"

Morty sat back in his chair. "I don't know," he
admitted. "All I do know is what I've already told
you."

Dover nodded. "And it's appreciated, but it
doesn't seem likely. It's too bad the government's
so secretive about its classified scientists. If he
doesn't volunteer information, there's not much we
can do about it."

The meeting dragged on for another hour. Sup-
positions and suspicions were brought up, but, ultimately, resulted in nothing. The only thing they
did agree on was that New Idea had to do something
about its electrical system and fast, before anything
else occurred.

After the meeting, Morty offered Sarah a ride
home. She took him up on it, wanting to talk more
about Sin.

"I'm sorry I had to say what I did about Sin,"
Morty told her as he drove. "But in a case like this,
we have to get all the evidence out in the open."

"I accept that," she conceded. "But as much as

you think he's responsible, I know in my heart that he's not.''

''Maybe,'' Morty said diplomatically. ''Sarah, I have more to say, and I want you to listen to me with an open mind.''

She took a deep breath. ''I know you think you're doing this for my own good, but—''

''Just give me five minutes, then I'll never bring up the subject again unless you ask me to,'' he broke in. When she agreed, he pulled over to the side of the road and looked at her intently. ''I've talked this over with Seamus Pornaygun and we've both come to the same conclusions.''

''Which are?''

Morty paused. ''Before I go on, I want you to know that Seamus and I have put a lot of thought into this. We're not ones to make accusations lightly. We've analyzed—''

Sarah couldn't take any more of his waffling. ''Morty, enough already!'' she snapped. ''Get on with it!''

''Right,'' he said, and began. ''There have been a number of things that are too coincidental to be coincidence, including the items I discussed at the meeting. Why was Sin at the car accident so quickly? What is his background? What was he doing near the camera? How come the intruder knew about your pyrophobia?''

"We went over all that with Johnny and Dover," Sarah reminded him, unhappy to rehash these questions.

"Yes, we did, but there's more." Morty was so serious he began to frighten her. "Although he didn't care at first, Seamus eventually saw there was a problem and got involved. He tried to draw Sin out, but every time he did, Sin managed to change the subject. Also, Seamus has one of the nation's highest security clearances, yet he's also denied access to Sin's files. In fact, he was even ordered never to ask about it again."

"That shouldn't be unusual for such a classified project," she said.

"It shouldn't, but I started thinking along a different line." Morty looked as if he was sorry for what was about to come. "Sarah, what were you and Sin talking about that night he stopped to help the raccoon?"

Sarah thought. "Nothing earth shattering, if I remember correctly."

"Well, you don't. You told me at the time that you were discussing Sin's background. Don't you see? As soon as anyone starts digging, he does anything he can to change the subject. Think about it."

Sarah realized Morty was right. Before they found the raccoon, she had just told Sin that she didn't know much about Ron's background and had asked him about his own.

"You're right," she admitted. "But that doesn't change the fact that his background is classified."

"No, it doesn't. It does bring up another point, though. It's one I'm not happy to make."

Sarah sighed. "You've gone this far—why stop now?"

"Whoever is responsible for these break-ins has to have a specific reason in mind," Morty continued. "As I said at our first meeting with Dover, it might not be just to steal things—it could be to ruin New Idea's reputation. If word were to leak out that we couldn't provide proper security, our large contracts would leave, probably overnight."

"That's possible," Sarah agreed. "Why are you telling me this now, though? Why didn't you bring it up with Dover?"

"Because I want you to investigate that possibility without interference from either the police or the government."

Sarah wasn't sure where this was heading. "Don't you trust them?"

"No, I don't. If there wasn't something suspicious going on, we'd have access to those classified files. Whatever they're not telling us can't be for the good of New Idea. But that's not my reason for wanting *you* to investigate. It occurred to me that whoever's trying to infiltrate New Labs would need the help of someone inside, preferably someone on the security staff.''

''You suspect Johnny?'' Sarah asked tentatively.

Morty shook his head. ''No, Sarah,'' he said sadly. ''I'm referring to you.''

''Me?'' Sarah was shocked. That was nothing compared to what came next.

''Sarah,'' Morty went on, ''I believe Sin has shown interest in you so that he would have an inside source on the security staff.''

''That's preposterous!'' Sarah exploded. ''Sin and I are very much in love. As a matter of fact, we were just talking about his working here on a full-time basis after the Pornaygun project is over!''

''I hope I'm wrong, but don't you think there's at least a possibility that I'm right?'' he asked.

''No.''

''Fine,'' Morty challenged, ''then prove me wrong.''

She glared at him. ''That's just what I intend to do.''

Chapter Eleven

"All the world loves a clown," the clown said, and squirted Sin with water from a flower in his lapel. Sarah laughed, and the clown squirted her too.

"Now *that's* funny," Sin said with a chuckle as the clown bowed, made a rather rude noise, and walked away.

"It was funnier when it happened to you." Sarah wiped herself off, then waved at Dr. Pornaygun, who was coming over with Ron.

"It's a grand day for a party," the doctor said, a twinkle in his eye. "It certainly was nice of New Idea to throw this shindig. Things have been getting a bit tense lately, and this is just the thing to pick up our spirits."

Sarah nodded in agreement. Despite everything, she felt very happy today. She had to give credit to the board. They had sensed the atmosphere and decided to throw a barbecue on the huge lawn to improve morale. It was an idea that was working very well.

"It's nice to get out of that lab for a while," Ron said. "My boss is a real slave driver."

"He's awful," Sin agreed.

"And bound to get worse if he hears any more talk like that from you two hoodlums!" Pornaygun wagged his finger at the pair and they all laughed.

"Attention!" a voice called over the loudspeaker. "All contestants for the egg toss, please come to the barbecue area."

Sin turned to Sarah. "What do you say?"

She laughed. "I don't think so."

"How about you and Ronnie competing?" Dr. Pornaygun said to Sin. "The two of you can represent our lab and make me proud."

Sarah sensed that Pornaygun wanted to talk to her alone. "That's a great idea," she said, wanting to get everything out in the open.

Sin didn't seem to agree, but Ron didn't give him a chance to protest. "For the honor of our lab!" he exclaimed, giving a gladiator's salute. "Besides, it won't be the first time I've had egg on my face."

Sin kissed Sarah on the cheek; then he and Ron left to join the other contestants.

"Take a walk with me, Sarah," Pornaygun said, and the two strolled away from the festivities. When they were off by themselves, Pornaygun resumed talking. "Morty told me he spoke to you a few days ago about what he and I had discussed. I just want to make sure that he expressed my feelings correctly."

Sarah said nothing.

"I hope you're not too mad at us for thinking that Sin might be using you," he said apologetically. "I want you to know that I've changed my mind a bit since then. He may have started out with an ulterior motive, but I truly believe he's in love with you now."

She knew that Pornaygun, like Morty, was doing what he thought best, but it still irritated her. "Then what's the problem?" she asked, keeping her temper in check.

"The problem is that strange things are still going on in our lab. We should be finished with our work by now, but little things have happened that keep throwing us off schedule. It's nothing I can prove, but it's suspicious nevertheless."

"And, of course, you think Sin's involved." Sarah's high spirits were quickly fading away.

"There's just so much going against him," the doctor explained. "The people he worked with are all either dead or unavailable. The university he claims he went to has his transcript, but no other records." Pornaygun took her hand. "I'm only telling you this so you know to be careful. You know how much—''

"Dr. Pornaygun," Sarah said coldly, her temper getting the better of her as she pulled away from him, "let me assure you that I am a professional. If Sin is doing something wrong, I will see to it that the appropriate actions are taken regardless of my feelings for him."

Pornaygun looked downhearted. "I'm sorry you're upset with me. I wish it didn't have to be this way."

"So do I."

Without another word, they went back to where the egg toss had begun. Ron and Sin did well and were one of two pairs left, when Sin botched a toss and the egg broke on his sneaker. They both came back good-naturedly blaming each other for the loss.

"If you knew how to catch, we would have won!" Ron said with mock indignity.

"You call that a toss? My sister could throw better than that!" Sin shot back in the same vein.

They all laughed, and then Dr. Pornaygun put his arm around Ron's shoulders and walked off with him, saying that he wanted to show him something on the other side of the lawn.

Sarah handed Sin some tissues so he could wipe off his sneaker. "I never knew you had a sister," she said.

"Huh?" He looked at her strangely.

"You said you had a sister."

"I never said any such thing!" he snapped.

"You said your sister could throw better than Ron." She was suspicious of the way he had reacted to her statement. "I didn't mean anything by it."

"Oh, that." Sin laughed, although it obviously wasn't genuine. "I was just kidding around."

Sarah had brought up the subject in the hope it might lead into a discussion of Sin's family. Now she was sorry she'd asked, but she still felt the need to play out her charade. "Then you don't have a sister?"

"I already told you that my only living relative is an aunt," he replied. "I would have mentioned a sister long before this."

"I know," she said. "It's just that I don't know much about your background."

Sin's eyes held her gaze. "Such as?"

She fidgeted as she spoke—part acting, part real nervousness. "Like where you were born, where did you grow up, did you have any girlfriends. . . . " She was interrupted by his laughter, this time very real.

"I see what this is all about! You're afraid that there might be somebody else in my life." He smiled and raised his right hand while putting his left over his heart. "I, Sinclair Edwards, do solemnly swear that the only girl in my life is Sarah Phillips and I pledge my undying loyalty to her.''

''You don't have to go that far.'' Sarah actually giggled and was very surprised at how fast her good humour returned when she was around him. How could what Morty and Pornaygun said be true? She so wanted to believe that it wasn't.

''I want to,'' he said. ''I've never met anyone else like you, and I don't ever want to lose you.''

She only had to look into his eyes to know she felt the same. ''I don't want to lose you, either,'' she whispered. They kissed, and nothing else seemed to matter to her any longer.

''Hey!'' Ron yelled over to them. ''This is a family picnic!'' They broke their embrace, both turning a bit red.

''We'd better get back to the picnic,'' Sin told her. ''You've made quite a scene here already.''

''*I've* made a scene?'' She hit him in the arm.

''Yes, you.'' He looked at his watch as he rubbed his arm. ''Uh-oh. I hate to say this, but isn't it time for you to relieve Johnny?''

She looked at her own watch and groaned. ''You're right. Duty calls.''

''I'll walk you back.'' He took her hand in his, and they went to the recently repaired front doors. ''I'll stay with you.''

"I'd like that, but you'd better not. Morty's in there too, and . . . ." She shrugged.

"I understand." He kissed her good-bye.

She went into the lab, only to find that Sin was right behind her. "One more." He took her in his arms once again. Her eyes closed, and she dreamed that this moment would last forever.

"See you later," Sin said.

"Count on it," she whispered, slowly opening her eyes. Suddenly a chill swept through her. His outline was silhouetted against the outside light. She recognized the same figure she had seen the night of the break-in! She stood there staring after him.

Upon seeing her standing motionless, Morty came over. "What's the matter, Sarah?" he asked.

"Nothing," she said, but it was obvious that she wasn't being truthful.

"Did you find out something?"

"No, I. . . . " Another thought raced through her mind, further adding to her fears. Once again, Sin had steered the conversation away from questions about his background.

"What's the matter with you?" Morty asked, obviously concerned.

"Morty," she said, fighting very hard to keep from crying, "you may be right about Sin."

"What changed your mind?"

"Nothing that I want to talk about until I'm sure

it's true,'' she said, drawing on an inner strength she never knew she possessed. "All right, now that I'm as suspicious as you are, how do I go about proving any of it?''

Morty scratched his head. "I'm not sure. Do you remember anything Sin said that we might be able to check up on?''

"He told me his only living relative was an aunt, but I don't have any idea what her name is or where she lives. Let me think. . . . " She tried to remember all their time together. She started at the hospital, then the amusement park, and . . . . "I remember something." She closed her eyes and concentrated so she would get it right. "There was a man at the amusement park who said he knew Sin from their days at Dynamic Computers. He called Sin 'Josh' and spoke about the plant closing a couple of years ago.''

"Do you remember the man's name?'' Morty asked.

"Yes . . . it was Burton. No, that wasn't it.'' She thought hard, then looked up at Morty. "It was Barton, Robby Barton!''

Morty smiled. "Good work, Sarah. This might be the key we need to figure out what's going on around here. I'll find out all I can about Dynamic Computers, and then I'll visit Robby Barton.''

"No, you won't.''

"What?" Morty was taken aback. "You don't think I should check up on this?"

She shook her head. "*I* should."

Since she had carried her overnight bag on the plane, Sarah didn't have to follow the crowd to the baggage area at the airport. Instead, she went directly to the auto-rental area where a car was ready and waiting, as promised. Following the directions Morty had given her, she headed for Robby Barton's house.

As she drove, she went over all the information Morty had uncovered about Dynamic Computers. Up until two years ago, Dynamic had been one of the hottest companies in the computer industry. It had grown from a small, basement firm to a major conglomerate that sold parts and software all over the world.

A year before its demise, the company quite unexpectedly had run into fiscal problems. There were all sorts of allegations, the main one being that top management was somehow spiriting funds away. Nothing was ever proved and the company was eventually taken over and sold off piece by piece.

The particular piece near where Barton lived had been the corporate headquarters and original factory. For some reason, it had never been sold off. That was all Sarah knew.

The ride wasn't long, and she soon found herself

in front of the Barton house. In her mind, she went over the story she and Morty had concocted. Though she was excited to go on a "mission" such as this, she hated the reason it had to be done. Thoughts of Sin came into her mind, and before they could interfere, she got out of the car and walked across the toy-strewn yard to the front door.

When she rang the bell, a young boy answered. He reminded her of the boys she had saved from the fire, and again she had to put the thoughts out of her mind. The boy left, calling for his father, and Barton soon appeared.

"Can I help you?" he asked, looking at her with a puzzled expression. "Don't I know you?"

Sarah had hoped he would recognize her, but was prepared if he didn't. "Yes," she said, "we met at the amusement park when you were visiting your in-laws a few weeks ago."

Barton thought for a moment, and then his round face opened up in a big smile. "Of course! You're the woman with Josh Charles! There's nothing wrong, is there?"

Inwardly Sarah was happy to obtain "Josh's" whole name, but outwardly she was sad as she embarked on the next phase of data gathering.

"I'm afraid there is." She bowed her head. "Josh has been in an accident. He's in a coma."

"No!" Barton's eyes grew misty, and he looked

so upset that she had to hold herself in from telling him the truth.

"Mr. Barton," she continued, "I'm hoping you can help me. Josh never said much about his days at Dynamic Computers. I'd like to know if you can remember anything about him. The doctors say that if we talk to him about things from the past, he might come out of it."

"I'll help in any way I can," Barton said. He held the door open for her with one hand, while pulling out a handkerchief with the other. One terrific nose blow later, he ushered her into his kitchen.

After two hours of carefully steered conversation, Sarah found out that Josh Charles had been brought into Dynamic Computers as a troubleshooter to find out what was going wrong with the company. He had been a friendly fellow, but kept to himself. There were no incidents of major significance. Josh Charles sounded as if he could be Sin, but his description and actions were so vague, he could have been any number of men.

Eventually, Sarah saw that their conversation was going around in circles, so she got the names of some other people who had worked at Dynamic. She gave Barton the name of her hotel, in case he remembered anything else, then left to search out the others.

By the end of the day, Sarah found out that the information Barton had given her had been the most useful of all. Everyone had something nice to say about Josh Charles, but no one knew much about him or his background. He had been at Dynamic only a few months before the company was sold, and she couldn't help but wonder if he had anything to do with the sale.

Sarah checked into her hotel, and as she started to settle down the phone rang. It was Morty, and she told him what she had found.

"I'll run some checks on Josh Charles, but I'll be surprised if we find anything dramatic," he said. "From what you tell me, we can't be sure of anything. It might just be a case of mistaken identity."

"If only someone who worked at Dynamic had kept—" Sarah was interrupted by a knock at her hotel door. She told Morty to hold on, then went to find Robby Barton and his two children standing there.

"Sorry to disturb you," he said, looking sheepish, "but there's something I want to give you. I found it in a drawer, and seeing how much in love the two of you obviously are, I thought you should have it." He handed her an envelope and then his kids took off down the hall. "I'd better be going. Good luck to both of you." He ran off after his children.

Sarah closed the door and opened the envelope. Inside was a picture of Robby Barton . . . and Sin.

There was no denying it now. She went back to the phone.

"What was that all about?" Morty asked.

"Nothing," she replied. "I'll see you tomorrow." She hung up, then spent the rest of the night staring at the picture and crying.

Chapter Twelve

Sarah wished she could run and hide when she saw Ron's car pulling into the parking lot. Since returning from her investigative trip that morning, she had managed to avoid everyone. Morty, Pornaygun, and Sin had all left messages on her answering machine, but Sarah didn't respond to any of them. She knew she'd see them soon enough, and she wanted to have the hours before her shift to think things out. It didn't really help, though. She had spent all that time staring at the picture Robby Barton had given her. She had even brought it to work, hiding it under the phone.

Ron was whistling and happy as he strode to the front door. He knew the camera was on him and did a little dance that caused Sarah to smile regardless of how she felt. He continued the dance all the way down the corridor, ending with a flourish and a big "ta-dah!" as he got to the command center.

"Very nice." Sarah clapped as Ron steadied himself against the console. He was breathing heavily and motioned for a glass of water, which she gave him hastily. "Are you all right?" she asked, concerned.

"I'm fine," he managed to stammer between gulps. "Do you mind if I sit down for a second?"

"Here." She offered him her chair, even though she wanted to send him on his way. He didn't look good as he sat there. "Are you sure you're all right?"

"I'm sure," he said. "We've been working such long hours, I suppose I'm a lot more exhausted than I thought. I'll be glad when this project is finished."

"You and me both," Sarah mumbled.

"What's that?"

"Nothing. Do you feel any better?"

"I feel great." He laughed, then abruptly turned serious. "Say, how are *you* doing? Morty said you weren't here yesterday because you were a little under the weather. I hope you're feeling okay."

"I am," she said. "Thanks for asking."

"No, you're not." Ron looked at her closely. Sarah wished he would leave, but he gave no indication of doing so. "Something's bothering you, and I think I know what it is. Obviously, it has to do with Sin. Everyone knows our project is coming to an end and he'll be leaving soon. You're upset about that."

"You guessed it," Sarah said, deciding to go along with him.

"No, I didn't." Ron surprised her not only by his statement but by the fact that his perpetual smile had vanished. "Sarah, it's time you and I had a talk. I know things that you should know, and I'm sure you know things that I should. Events are coming to a head here, and I don't want to see you get hurt."

"What are you talking about?" she asked, perplexed.

He looked at her intently. "I think you know. You're not the only one working on this. I'm here, and I—"

A slight buzz interrupted, and both of them looked to the screen to see Sin entering the facility. As if someone had flicked a switch, the smile returned to Ron's face.

"We'll talk more later," he whispered to her, then looked at the arriving Sin and said in a loud voice, "Ladies and gentlemen, here he is now! He's the baron of biology, the king of chemistry, the one, the only, Sinclair Edwards! Let's have a big hand for him, folks!"

Sin paid Ron no attention, coming directly up to Sarah. "How are you?" he asked her. "I phoned, but you never returned my calls. I'm sorry I couldn't come over, but Pornaygun wouldn't let me out of the lab. I hope you know—"

"Enough!" Ron interrupted. "She's fine, Sin, and we've got work to do."

Sin whirled on the other man. "I'll be right with you, Ron," he snapped. "Give me a minute, will you?" It was more an order than a question.

Ron stood up, a visible wave of anger passing over him. Sarah jumped in between them, momentarily afraid they might come to blows, but Ron's tenseness passed. "Sorry, Sin," he said. "All those hours we've been putting in have made me a little edgy. You and Sarah take all the time you need." He turned and went to the lab.

"What's going on with you, Sarah?" Sin asked.

"I don't want to talk about it," she said, and immediately was sorry she had said anything. "At least not right now."

"Then when? If there's something wrong between us, I want to make it right. I don't want to lose what we have."

Ordinarily, a statement like that would have made her feel as if she were floating on a cloud. Now it only added to her uneasiness.

"Sin, there isn't—" She was interrupted by the ringing phone.

"Say 'Hi, Morty,' and then listen carefully to what I'm about to tell you," a voice, which she recognized as Ron's, instructed.

"Hi, Morty," she replied, holding the earpiece as close as possible without being obvious.

"Tell him to wait a second," Sin said sternly.

"Do what he wants," Ron put in, and Sarah put her hand over the receiver.

"I have to get to work, but you and I need to talk," Sin said, his eyes on her. "I don't know if. . . . No, I *will* get off for an hour or so, and you and I can get together then."

"All right," she replied, and he walked toward his lab. She got back on the phone.

"Is he still there?" Ron asked, a tone of urgency in his voice.

"He just left."

"Then I'll make this brief. I have to talk to you about Sin as soon as possible. We're working on a common problem here, Sarah, and we've got to pool our information and come up with a solution before it's too late!"

"What's going on?"

"I can't tell you now, but I could be the man who saves your life. Have to go." The line went dead.

Sarah thought about her conversation with Ron long into the night. She came up with no answers and was very anxious when Ron finally came out of the lab.

"I'm going to the lounge," he said in passing.

"Pick up the phone when I call and we'll have a talk. It'll have to be short, though. Sin's waiting for me to come back so *he* can talk with you."

She nodded and he went down to the lounge. A million thoughts swept through her mind as she waited for the phone to sound. She picked it up on the first ring.

"We only have a few minutes, so I'm going to have to talk fast," Ron said. "Can you see me?"

She turned on the lounge camera. "I can," she replied.

"Good." He pulled a card out of his wallet and held it up to the camera. She could see it was government identification. "I'm a Federal agent. I've been assigned to this lab to protect it from espionage."

Sarah didn't want to waste time asking questions, so she remained silent and let him continue.

"I'm here for three reasons," he explained. "First off, to work on Pornaygun's project. I am a scientist, and not a bad one at that. Second, I'm here to safeguard the experiment against any possible intrusions. Third, I'm here to keep an eye on Sin. We don't know exactly who he is or what he's doing here, but we do know he's trouble. This isn't the first time he's attempted something like this, but you already know that."

"What do you mean?"

"Dynamic Computers," Ron said. "We know all about your trip there."

"How could you?" she asked suspiciously. "Have you been spying on me?"

"Yes," he admitted. "With a project that has implications like this one does, everyone is under suspicion."

"Then you know I didn't find out much," she said, a bit angry that she had been watched.

"We know your suspicions of Sin were enough to make you follow the clues you found. You're a very resourceful person. If you ever want an agency job, you'll get my endorsement."

"Thanks a bunch."

"Let's get to the point," Ron said. "What we know is that Sin is here to endanger either the project or New Idea itself. We do have a vague idea who he is. I don't want to see you get hurt. Personally, though, I don't think that would ever happen."

Once again, Sarah was not quite sure what was going on. All she knew was that she and Sin would never be together. "Explain that to me, Ron," she said, forcing down the lump in her throat.

Ron sighed. "I genuinely believe that Sin has fallen in love with you." He smiled at her broadly on screen. "It's not a hard thing to do—I almost did it myself. Anyway, I think that his love has kept you from harm during the break-ins."

"So now what? Are you going to order me to stop seeing him for the sake of my country?"

"I can't order that, but I would recommend it. Although I'm sure you don't believe it, Sin is a dangerous man. If he's pushed hard enough, even your love might not be enough to save you."

"I can handle myself," Sarah insisted.

"You've proved that many times over," Ron agreed, "but we're not talking about your run-of-the-mill criminal here. Sin is a trained professional and will stop at nothing to achieve his goal. I wish I could take him into custody now, but we have to find out exactly what he's up to and who he's working for."

The other line rang and Sarah put Ron on hold to answer it. Sin's voice came through, wanting to know where Ron was. She said she thought he was in the lounge and would tell him to go back to the lab. Sin told her he'd come talk to her as soon as Ron returned, then hung up. Sarah informed Ron of the conversation.

"I'd better get back before he gets suspicious," he said. "Remember everything I told you, Sarah, and be careful! Never let on what you know, especially about Sin. It could save your life."

He hung up and quickly returned to his lab. Sin exited as Ron entered, which gave Sarah no time at all to think things over.

"What's going on?" Sin asked. He came up to face her around the other side of the command center.

"What do you mean?" she asked, not wanting to divulge anything.

He threw his hands up in exasperation. "You don't come to work, no one can find you, and you treat me like I'm a total stranger!" His voice rose as he spoke. "What's bothering you?"

She turned away from him, trying to prevent the anger within her from rising to the surface. "It's nothing."

"No. It's obviously something, and it's affecting our relationship. Tell me what it is."

"Just leave me alone," she whispered. Fury and rage caused by her aching heart came closer and closer to exploding out of her. She tried her mental exercises.

"Sarah, I've been honest with you . . ." he began, and, finally, she could hold it in no longer.

"Honest!" She stood up to face him, her body trembling with emotion. "Come on! You haven't spoken honestly since the day we met!"

Sin looked at her blankly. "What are you talking about?"

She tried to control her voice. "Do you really and truly believe you've been honest with me?"

"Yes, I have. I don't know what's bothering you, but, whatever it is, I'm sure we can work it out."

Sarah said nothing, and then it was his turn to explode. "This is completely irrational!" He reached over and grabbed her shoulders, as if to shake the answers from her. Sarah grimaced, and he quickly let go, his anger subsiding.

"Sin," she said slowly, trying to regain control of the situation, "I just don't want to see you anymore." The words hurt her as much as they seemed to hurt him.

"Why?" Disappointment was written all over his face, and Sarah wondered if it was an act. "Is there someone else?"

And there it was—her way out of the situation. "Yes," she said softly. Her very soul churned as her dream of their life together vanished forever.

"I don't believe you. There can't—" A buzzing interrupted them, and Johnny came through the front doors. They both regarded him coolly.

"Is there some sort of problem here?" he asked.

"No," Sarah told him.

"Yes, there is," Sin contradicted her. His eyes pinned Johnny down with a threatening glare. "Give us a few minutes alone, Johnny."

"Whatever," he said, remembering what had happened the last time Sin gave him that look. He left for the lounge.

Sarah sighed, fervently wishing this would be over soon. She didn't know how much more she could bear. "Sin, I—" she began, then the phone rang and she picked it up. Ron was on the other end.

"Is Sin still there?" he asked, and Sarah said yes. "Put him on the line."

Sin took the phone from her and listened for a moment. "All right," he said, then came around to her side of the command center to hang up the phone. "We have more talking to do. This can't be over between us, at least not like this."

She shook her head. "I'm sorry, but it is over."

"No!" Sin slammed the phone down on its base. The whole command center shook with the power of his anger . . . and the picture Sarah had hidden underneath the phone was revealed.

"That's mine," she said. She quickly reached over to pick it up, but Sin was faster. He took only a second to examine it before he placed it in his pocket.

"I strongly suggest you keep this to yourself." His tone was icy. "It'll be for your own good."

"Sin, let's go!" Ron called, coming down to the command center. "I need your help."

"We'll talk more later," Sin whispered to her, and then left with Ron.

Shortly thereafter, Johnny came to relieve her and Sarah hurriedly left New Idea. She stopped off to have a cup of coffee, hoping it would calm her down and allow her to gather her thoughts. It did neither and she went home, wondering what to do next. Dejectedly, she walked into her apartment building . . . to find Sin waiting for her.

"I'm not going to hurt you," he said, as though reading her thoughts. "But we do have to talk."

Sarah debated what to do. It might be possible to run from the building before he reached her, but that would only mean a future confrontation probably a lot more nasty than this. The only real choice was to listen to him and hope that Ron had been right about Sin really caring for her. In silence, they made their way to her apartment, where he sat in an easy chair. She sat on the couch across from him, quickly formulating a number of plans should he attack her.

"I'm listening," she told him warily.

"Good." He smiled at her, but that only made her angry, considering the new nature of their relationship. "Sarah, this whole thing has gone too far."

"What does that mean?" She didn't know how to interpret his statement. Was it a threat?

"It means that I've been careless. I've let my feelings interfere with my work, and that's put both of us in a rather awkward situation."

She could take the suspense no longer. "Sin—if that's your real name—what exactly is going on here? And what are you going to do to me?"

He stood up slowly and came over to her. Despite herself, she flinched. "There's no need for you to be scared," he said, his eyes holding hers. "I've never lied to you, by either word or deed, about my feelings for you. Unfortunately, who I am and what I'm doing will have to remain my secret. All you have to know is that I'd never do anything to hurt you or the people at New Idea."

"Unless you have to." She looked away, her worst fears confirmed.

He touched her cheek gently. "No, I would never do anything to hurt you. In your heart you know that's true."

"I don't know anything about you anymore," she said, angry at what had become of their relationship.

"I wish I could answer your questions."

"If you can't, then why did you come here?"

He drew in a deep breath. "Two reasons. The first is to tell you that I love you and I always will. Sarah, you—"

"And the second reason?" she interrupted. What he was saying hurt too much to be continued.

"The second reason," he said, his voice touched with hurt, "is to warn you not to tell anyone what you've found out. Someday you'll see why, but for now do what I say. You don't know what you're dealing with."

"Is that all?" Sarah asked, hoping this was the end of their conversation.

"Yes."

"Then please leave. But first, I have a warning for you." Somehow she managed to keep her voice devoid of any emotion. "If I catch you doing anything to hurt New Idea, or anyone in it, I'll do everything in my power to stop you."

"Fair enough," he said, and with a sad look headed for the door. "I'll always love you, Sarah."

Tears flowed freely down her cheeks as she watched him go. "And I'll love you too," she whispered. "Always."

Chapter Thirteen

Sarah's moods fluctuated from bad to worse over the next few days. Morty, who had been hired back as a consultant since the last break-in, realized something was definitely wrong. He had also seen that she had been avoiding Sin and didn't even acknowledge his presence when they passed each other in the hall. He had not broached the subject, but instead had tried to keep things light.

Morty's heart went out to Sarah as he saw her sitting dejectedly at the command center. Although he had a few more places to check for the installation of a new security system, he went over to her.

"You can't be sad for the rest of your life," he said, and she looked up at him with a half smile.

"I know, Morty. I'm trying, but it's so hard."

He gave her a hug. "You'll be fine," he said, comforting her. "Once this experiment is over,

165

they'll all be out of here and you'll see how easy it is to forget."

"I hope so." She sighed and patted his hand.

"Great." He smiled at her warmly. "Have you looked over the proposal I've made for the new system?"

"Yes, but I haven't made any comments yet. I've seen Johnny's analysis, though, and he's been pretty rough on it."

"That's about what I'd expect."

Ron came striding over, his eyes bleary and his face pale. "Hello, security people," he said with a yawn. "I can't tell you how happy I'll be once this experiment is over. I can't remember the last time I got a decent amount of sleep."

"Taking a break?" Sarah asked, worrying that Sin would be right behind.

"A short one," he answered. "We're coming up to a critical point and we have to be fresh for it."

"Then you'd better be about your business," Morty put in.

"Sure will." He indicated the copy of Morty's report. "Still having trouble with the security system?"

"Nothing for you to worry about," Morty said very authoritatively. "Sarah's here, and I'm here, and that's all we need."

Ron smiled and went on his way.

"You don't think there'll be any trouble, do you?" she asked. He didn't know about Sin and Ron, but she wanted his reassurance nevertheless.

Morty shook his head. "No, but you never can be too careful." He opened his jacket to reveal a small gun holstered in his belt.

Sarah was astonished. "Morty!" she cried.

"Shh!" he quickly closed his jacket. "It's nothing unusual—I've been carrying it since I began to work here. This is just the first time you ever saw it."

"You still shouldn't carry it." Movement caught her eye. She looked to the screen and saw Sin heading their way. "Morty, would you mind taking over for a while? I have to go . . . powder my nose."

"Sure," he said, and Sarah was gone by the time Sin rounded the corner. She knew that Morty wouldn't tell him where she was.

She spent some extra time in the women's room, in case Sin had deduced where she was. Even so, she still didn't come out until she opened the door a crack and made sure no one was in the lounge. Breathing a sigh of relief, she took a few steps, but that breath caught in her throat as Sin came out of the shadows.

"What do you want?" she asked, frightened.

"I want you to go home now!" he ordered. "Don't argue with me, don't call anyone, don't say anything. Just get in your car and leave!"

"Sin, if you're—"

"Quiet!" He listened for something that Sarah couldn't hear. "I have to go. Now do what I've told you and get out of here." He took her in his arms and kissed her before she could stop him. "I love you, Sarah Phillips." Then he was gone.

She stared after him, her mind in complete confusion. Before she even had time to wonder what was going on, she heard a noise behind her. She turned to see Ron coming out of the men's room. He didn't look happy.

"You heard?" she asked.

He nodded, his face grim. "Why did he tell you that? You didn't tell him about me, did you?"

"No," she said gloomily, "but he did find a picture I had of him and Robby Barton."

Ron threw up his hands. "How could you do that?" he snapped.

"I didn't do it on purpose!" she snapped back.

"Well, at least we can be thankful that's the only thing he knows," Ron said. "Something big must be about to happen for him to approach you like that."

Sarah had had enough. "Ron, this has gone too far. I'm going to call the police." She went over and picked up the lounge phone, only to find there was no dial tone. "It's not working!"

Ron scowled. "Then we have to move fast. Sarah, I'm counting on you to do everything I say if we're going to make it through this."

"What do we do first?"

"I'll go out and check if Sin's in the lab," Ron said quickly. "If he's not, I'll warn Pornaygun. I want you to find Morty and tell him everything that's happened. After that, one of you go for help and the other join me at the lab. Understand?"

She nodded, "but what if he *is* out there?"

"Then I'll do whatever I have to, to safeguard the project." The grim comment sent shivers down her spine. "Be careful, Sarah."

Ron went out, closing the door behind him. A few moments later, she heard him call Sin's name, followed by the sound of a heavy body falling against the lounge door. Sarah cracked the door open, and was very surprised to find no one there. She opened it farther and stuck her head out. From the corner of her eye she caught a sudden movement and turned to face it. That was the last thing she saw.

"We're waiting for you," one of the flame-covered boys called out to her.

"And we're going to get you very, very soon!" the other said. Then they both began to laugh, and laugh, and laugh . . . .

* * *

Sarah screamed and sat bolt upright, the fire dream fading and dizziness setting in. Her head throbbed with pain, and she discovered a tender lump on the side of her skull.

Slowly and shakily, she got to her feet. Someone had knocked her out, but whoever it was seemed to be gone. She looked at her watch to see how long she had been unconscious. Panic set in as she realized she could barely see in front of her. Had the blow partially blinded her?

It took another second before she saw that only the auxiliary lights were on, their dim glow barely illuminating the place. She finally focused on her watch, and estimated that only ten minutes had elapsed since she was in the lounge.

She staggered over to the command center. There was no sign of Morty, and he didn't answer when she whispered for him.

She tried the command-center phone, but it was as dead as the one in the lounge. She tried the screens, but all the equipment was down. Only the emergency generator seemed to be working, and that just barely. There was no way to call out and no way for anyone outside to call in.

Sarah knew what she had to do. Cautiously, she made her way down the corridors to Dr. Pornaygun's lab. She hoped nothing bad had happened, but prepared for the worst. Her fears were realized as she approached the door of the lab.

A body, still and unmoving, lay outside the lab. It was Morty. Dropping down next to him, she felt for, and found, a pulse. Then, from inside the lab, she heard the sounds of a scuffle. She was about to open the door when Morty grabbed her by the arm.

"Sarah," he gasped. She had to put her ear to his mouth to hear him. "Ron . . . Sin . . . ."

"Don't try to talk," she whispered as soothingly as she could. Her eyes, now accustomed to the light, saw blood streaming down the side of his head. Morty's wound was serious, but not life-threatening. The sounds from the lab intensified, grabbing her attention, but Morty would not let go.

"Get out!" he whispered. "Call the police."

"I can't do that—it would take too long. I have to go in there."

"You're so stubborn." He pressed something cold into her hand, then passed out.

Sarah saw he had given her his gun. While she hated the need for it, the weapon was reassuring in her hand. She entered the computerized access code to the lab, which she knew but had never used. The door opened only partially, and she had to push all her weight against it until she made an opening big enough to enter through. She almost tripped as she walked inside, and she looked down to see Dr. Por-naygun's unconscious body blocking the door.

The lighting in the lab was no better than outside, but, even if it were pitch-black, the sounds of fighting pinpointed where the conflict was. Keeping a tight grip on the gun, she advanced to see Ron and Sin in what looked to be mortal combat.

"Stop it!" she yelled, getting as close as she could to the pair. They didn't listen. "I said stop it!" She aimed the gun in the air and fired off a shot. The sound echoed like a cannon, and the two men immediately stopped fighting. They looked at her in surprise.

"Good work, Sarah," Ron said, recovering quickly. "You've managed to stop this spy before he could make good with his plan."

Sin's mouth dropped. "Spy?" he said, disbelief in his voice. He turned to Sarah. "I'm a Federal agent—that's what I couldn't tell you all this time. I caught Ron stealing documents and wanted you to get out of here before any trouble started."

Now it was time for Ron's mouth to drop. "Don't listen to his lies. *I'm* the Federal agent, not this . . . imposter!"

Sin looked at Ron, then turned back to Sarah. "So that's what's going on. All right, I'll prove I'm who I say."

He reached into his jacket. As he did, Ron caught

him with a karate chop to the back of the neck. Sin crumbled to the ground. Ron came toward her, only to stop as Sarah aimed the gun squarely at his chest.

"Don't make another move," she ordered.

"What are you doing?" Ron asked. "He was going for a gun. Look, I'll prove it." He kept his hands in sight as he kicked open Sin's lab coat. A small gun was holstered under his arm.

"See?" Ron continued. But she still held Morty's gun on him. "Sarah, don't you understand? Sin was trying to use your love for him to make you believe that *he* was the agent."

Sarah's aim didn't waver, though her thoughts were jumbled. "I'm not sure what to believe," she said. "Until I am, we're going to stay just like this."

Ron's face grew red with anger. "Until when?" he snapped. "Until his henchmen arrive? We've got him down, now put you're feelings aside! You've done your job, now let me do mine."

Ron made sense, but if Sin were the agent. . . . "I just don't know. We're going to take this one step at a time."

"Then let's do it," Ron said with a sigh. "First, I'd like to show you my identification again. That will verify my identity."

"Okay, but do it slowly."

"Of course. I know the routine." He put up one hand, and used the other to slowly reach into his pocket. While he was reaching in, he quickly flexed and unflexed the fingers of the hand that was up in the air. Sarah's attention was momentarily distracted, and he used the moment to pull out a lighter. He clicked it on, and the flame danced wildly in the semidarkened room. Sarah's eyes focused on it— and wouldn't let go.

"Put it away," she whispered. She still held the gun steady, but stood frozen as Ron approached.

"Look at the flames, Sarah." Ron spoke monotonously, further hypnotizing her. "You've failed once again. You failed in the apartment building, didn't you? You saved those two brats, but what about the cost to you? What about that, Sarah Phillips?"

Suddenly, on both sides of the flame Ron was holding, the fire boys shimmered into existence.

"Ron brought us to take you away," one boy hissed, his arms outstretched toward her.

"You escaped us before," the other chimed in. *"Now you're ours!"*

"No," Sarah whispered, but she couldn't take her gaze off the flame, no matter how hard she tried.

"I really have to thank you for making this so easy for me," Ron said as he took the gun away from her. "I can't tell you how much fun it was to do all the things I did, then put the blame on Sin."

Sarah could say nothing as she fought her paralysis.

"But, I'm afraid, all good things must come to an end," Ron continued, his glee turning very solemn. "This truly has been a rewarding experience for me, so it's going to be tough to say good-bye. Let's prolong it a little, shall we? How about a little fire, Sarah?"

He brought up the lighter right in front of her face. Sweat poured out of her and her heart raced as he moved the lighter around. He laughed as he did, the fire boys laughing along with him in a symphony of sadism.

Suddenly, with a soul-wrenching scream, Sarah lashed out and knocked the lighter across the lab. It smashed into a row of fluid-filled beakers, which immediately began to burn. A stack of papers and computer disks that lay next to it were set aflame in turn.

"Oh, no!" Ron cried, and quickly got the fire extinguisher. He frantically tried to put the flames out, but the chemicals were immune to the foam. Sarah, her mental resistance to the fire completely gone after her attempt, watched in horror as the crimson boys grew until they crowded the room.

"Free!" they cried in terrible unison. "We're free!"

Ron, realizing the futility of his efforts, walked

back to her. "I wish you hadn't done that," he snapped. The smile returned to his face when he saw she still could not move. "That's life, I guess. If I can't get the notes to this experiment, the second best thing is knowing that, when those chemicals react, no one else will be alive to re-create it. You see, besides the fact that the work we were doing was top secret, the reason nobody was allowed in here was that this place is chock-full of flammable and explosive materials. Which reminds me—I'd better be going! Bye-bye!" He kissed her on the cheek. "It was nice knowing you."

Ron ran from the room as the flames continued to build. Somehow, Sarah managed to close her eyes, to try to drive out the sight of what was happening and to prevent the apartment-building scenario from returning. If it did, she had no chance at all. She concentrated on breaking out of her paralysis, but no matter how hard she tried, she couldn't drown out the voices in her head.

"This is all because of you!" they said, *their voices crackling and popping like the fire.*

"No," Sarah whispered, the boundaries of her mind beginning to close in.

"Morty . . . dead!"

"No!"

"Pornaygun . . . dead!"

"No!"

"Sin . . . dead!"

"No!"

"You killed them all!" they yelled, their laughter echoing throughout her very soul. "Because of you, they're all dead!"

"No! They won't die because of me!" she cried. "I won't let it happen!"

With a tremendous effort of will, from strength born of love, Sarah opened her eyes, and shook free of the paralysis that bound her. The flame boys were gone, but the fire was blazing worse than ever.

She quickly sized up the situation and found Ron had been right—there was no way to put out the fire. The first thing she had to do was get Sin and Dr. Pornaygun out and hope that the fire could be contained in the lab. Since Sin was in the fire's immediate path, he would be first. She grabbed him by the legs and pulled his massive frame to the doorway. He made no sound as she did, which worried her immensely.

"Sarah, what's going on?" a voice asked. She turned to see that Dr. Pornaygun had regained consciousness and had gotten to his feet shakily.

"There's no time for questions! The emergency systems are all down and we've got to get out of here before this whole place goes up!" she said to him as he struggled to regain his senses. "I want you to go outside and try to get help. I'll get Sin and Morty out of here.''

"And what about Ron?'' Pornaygun asked as he sadly saw his work being destroyed. "After what he did to me, and seeing this fire, I suppose he'd deserve it, but we can't just leave him here.''

"What are you talking about?'' Sarah asked, and Pornaygun pointed outside the lab. She saw Morty was still unconscious, and Ron, just as unmoving, was sprawled out next to him. He must have tripped over Morty on the way out. "I'll handle this,'' she said. "You just get out of here!''

Pornaygun took a step to help her, but his legs were wobbly and he knew he would only be another burden. "Good luck, Sarah!'' he said, and then stumbled down the corridor.

Sarah hurriedly pulled Sin from the room and closed the lab door shut behind her. The sounds of the advancing flames, along with a sharp series of small explosions, told her that the door wouldn't hold for long. Luckily, the ventilation system must have been partially open, because the fumes and smoke were not yet a threat. She stopped for a moment to catch her breath and decide what to do next.

There were three of them to get out, and she didn't think she'd have the time or strength to get more than one to safety. It was a horrible decision to have to make, but there was only one real choice. Ron had caused this, and that made him last, but of the other two . . . .

Without looking back, Sarah grabbed Morty by the legs and began to pull him away. Even though he was heavy, he weighed less than Sin, and she knew she could get him to safety even with the pain now beginning to flare up in her bad leg.

She had pulled Morty almost to the end of the corridor when an explosion rocked New Idea. She fell to the ground, twisting her leg, and sending bolts of pain ripping through her. With an effort, she put it out of her mind. She was about to get to her feet when a firm grip lifted her up. She turned to see Johnny, who had come to work surprisingly early. He never had looked so good.

"What's going on?" he asked, trying to make order out of the chaos. "Is anyone still back there?"

"Yes, Sin and Ron!" she yelled, as the sound of the approaching fire crackled louder. "We've got to—" Another explosion propelled her into Johnny, and they barely managed to stay on their feet. The corridor was now filled with small fires and the heat was becoming almost overwhelming.

"We've got to get out of here!" Johnny yelled at her. "This place could blow at any time! I called the fire department on my CB. They should be here soon—they'll rescue the others."

Sarah shook her head. "I can't leave Sin!" she cried.

"We have no choice! You've done all you could!" Johnny called back. She knew he was right, but that didn't matter.

"You go," she said, "and take Morty with you."

"Sarah, you can't—"

"I have to!" Before Johnny could stop her, she stumbled back down the corridor, using her arms to ward off the snapping flames.

Step by step, she fought her way forward until she reached the spot where Sin lay. The fire hissed all around, and she quickly put out the small flames that were burning his clothes. Sin was still unconscious, but his breathing was heavy. He appeared relatively unharmed. She grabbed hold of him under his arms, then felt a pressure on her leg. Looking down, she saw Ron grasping her ankle.

"Help me!" he cried, his voice raw. "I can't move my legs!"

"I can't take you both, Ron. The fire department is coming." She began to cough, the ventilation system no longer carrying the smoke outside. Ron only tightened his hold on her ankle.

"You can't leave me here!" he screamed.

"I'm sorry," she managed to say, and she kicked his hand off.

"No!" Ron roared. He took out Morty's gun and aimed it at her. "If I don't get out, none of us do!"

"Ron, you can't—" Another explosion interrupted them, knocking the gun out of Ron's hand. As he scrambled for it, she began to drag Sin away. He was dead weight, and that, added to the growing smoke and heat and her already weakened state, almost caused her to give up. Her love and determination drove her on. She hoped it was enough.

"Come back!" she heard Ron cry out, lost somewhere back in the smoke and flames. And then she heard him no more.

Sarah was almost at the end of her strength when she heard a groan. She looked down to make sure Sin was all right, and saw he was conscious.

"Sarah. . . . Leave me . . ." he said between coughs.

"I won't," she said, tears pouring from her already red eyes.

"Save yourself . . ." he pleaded, then fell back into unconsciousness.

"No!" Sarah cried, and, oblivious to the pain in her body and soul, she trudged forward. She didn't get much farther before it became too much and she sank to the ground with him.

"Where are you?" she heard a voice ask, and, through slitted eyes, saw shapes approaching. The flame boys—they were back! Then she realized the shapes weren't in her imagination, they were firemen in full fire gear!

"Sarah, is anyone else in there?" one of them asked, his muffled voice sounding very sweet. She blinked, and saw it was Captain Vincent behind the mask.

"Yes," she replied somewhat groggily. "One more. . . . " Then it all became too much for her and she passed out.

Chapter Fourteen

When Sarah woke up, she found herself in a hospital room. After a few moments of disorientation, she was able to make out a group of figures around her—doctors and nurses. She tried to speak to them, but all that came out was a cough. It did get their attention, and they gathered around, checking her with a variety of instruments.

She was weak, but felt little pain. From the staff's conversation, she found out that although she had been burned over much of her body, it was nothing serious or permanently debilitating. They soon left and Dr. Pornaygun entered.

"Dr. Pornaygun!" she cried, her voice hardly recognizable to herself. "What's going on?" She was more frightened now of what he might tell her happened in the fire than she had been during the experience itself.

"Calm down," he said as she struggled to sit up. Gently, he pushed her back down. "You shouldn't be surprised to see me—you did save my life, after all."

"I don't remember anything after I blacked out," she managed to say.

"You lost consciousness because of oxygen deprivation and exhaustion," he told her. "You've also suffered some nasty burns and reinjured your leg. Don't worry, though, it's not really bad. The doctors say you'll be good as new in no time at all."

"What about the fire?" she asked nervously.

"Well, most of New Idea burned down, but insurance will pay for repairs. By the time you're ready to go back to work, there should be something to go back to. Because of you, Johnny was able to get Morty to safety. He's fine, except for a lump on his head where Ron hit him. As for Ron, he'll get what he deserves."

"Then he's still alive?"

Pornaygun nodded. "Captain Vincent managed to get him out. It turns out Ron *is* a Federal agent who was working as a troubleshooter for a different branch of the government than Sin. They had never worked together before my project, as most experiments didn't call for both Ron's engineering background and Sin's computer skills.

"When they pulled him from the fire, Ron confessed not only to being behind everything that happened at New Idea but to a half-dozen other crimes as well. It seems he's been abusing his position and sabotaging projects for rival firms as well as selling secrets to the highest bidder. He provided a full list of names, but that won't help him avoid punishment. He's going away for a long, long time.''

Pornaygun saw that Sarah was looking at him eagerly, so he continued with his rundown of what had occurred while she had been unconscious.

''As far as my project goes, I don't have my notes any longer, but I've still got my brain.'' He tapped his forehead. ''That's all in the future, though. What matters right now is for you to get better. You saved all our lives, Sarah, and now it's our time to return the favor. That leaves us with just one more piece of business for the moment.'' He headed for the door.

Despite her anxiety over what the answer might be, Sarah couldn't hold herself in any longer. ''What about Sin?'' she called after him.

''Wait a minute,'' he said, and left the room. Her heart beat rapidly until Pornaygun returned. The doctor wheeled in a bandaged and bruised, yet smiling, man. It was Sin.

''The doctors say he can't stay here too long, so make the most of your time,'' Pornaygun said. He moved out of their way, grinning from ear to ear.

''Sarah, I was so worried about you,'' Sin said

hoarsely, and she saw tears well up in his eyes to match those already running down her face. "If you had died, I don't know what I'd have done."

"Don't talk that way," she said, and despite her bandages, she picked up his hand. "We're alive, and we're together."

"And that's the way it will be forever," he promised, his eyes dancing with joy.

"Forever," Sarah repeated dreamily as he leaned across to kiss her, "and ever. . . . ."